T0149582

The Tree That Knew Too Much

BY

VERN WESTFALL

THE TREE THAT KNEW TOO MUCH

iUniverse books may be ordered through booksellers or by contacting:

iUniverse
1663 Liberty Drive
Bloomington, IN 47403
www.iuniverse.com
1-800-Authors (1-800-288-4677)

Because of the dynamic nature of the Internet, any web addresses or links contained in this book may have changed since publication and may no longer be valid. The views expressed in this work are solely those of the author and do not necessarily reflect the views of the publisher, and the publisher hereby disclaims any responsibility for them.

Any people depicted in stock imagery provided by Thinkstock are models, and such images are being used for illustrative purposes only. Certain stock imagery © Thinkstock.

ISBN: 978-1-5320-1193-1 (sc)
ISBN: 978-1-5320-1194-8 (e)

Library of Congress Control Number: 2016919772

Print information available on the last page.

iUniverse rev. date: 11/29/2016

CHAPTER ONE

Floyd's annual pig roasts are special. They give me a day in the country and a day away from the responsibilities of being a lawyer. Floyd's doctor comes for the same reasons and brings his two sons. His wife stays at home. The roasts are too earthy for her. Floyd's father is always there, sitting in the same rusty lawn chair with his feet propped up on a tree stump. Floyd's minister comes, as do at least a dozen tradesmen. Floyd and his father are masons as well as farmers, and they have many friends.

The Brenner Farm is the perfect setting for Floyd's roasts. The farm has been in Floyd's family for three generations and has a much longer history. Indian relics are abundant and archeological digs have uncovered ice-age artifacts. Legends have also survived, passed down from Indian tribes to the first Ohio settlers and through them to Floyd's great grandfather. Floyd keeps the stories alive by re-telling them at every roast.

Floyd places his homemade barbeque between the barn and the old farmhouse where his grandmother lives. Grandma helps Floyd prepare but doesn't take part. She stays inside and peeks out from a side window.

Floyd lives with his parents in a new house on the other side of the farm. He and his father use county roads to drive around the farm every morning to check on grandma, have a cup of coffee, and tend the cattle. After morning farm chores, Floyd and his father load their work truck and spend a full day building basements and laying brick on local construction projects. After work, Floyd and his father check on grandma, settle the cattle, and drive back around the farm to his father's house for a late supper and a night's sleep.

Floyd's day starts before sun-up and lasts until dark. The work is hard. Floyd lifts concrete block all day and tosses bales of hay at night. He is six feet tall, wears suspendered overalls, has a scraggly black beard, and from a distance, he is an imposing figure. Up close, his smile and friendly manner reveal his true nature as a kind and gentle man.

Floyd is twenty-eight but has never dated and has no time to socialize. Except for his annual pig roasts, Floyd rarely takes a break. He never sleeps late and retires soon after supper, but today is different, today is party day and Floyd is enjoying himself. The guests have arrived, the pig has been roasting since dawn, the beer is cold and the tractor and flat bed wagon are ready for the hayride.

My name is David Perry and I have been the Brenner's lawyer for the past five years. I'm always invited to the roasts and I always attend. My ten-year old daughter, Jenny, would prefer to stay home and watch TV. She hates the sight of a whole animal roasting over hot coals and can't stand the smell of the barn, but she endures the sights and smells just to hear Floyd's stories, especially his stories about the tree.

To keep track of time at his roasts, Floyd ignores his digital watch and sequences events by observing the shadow cast by the barn's weathervane. When the shadow reaches the beer keg, Floyd knows it's time for the hayride. When it reaches the barbeque, he knows the pig is ready to serve.

This year's roast has the benefit of clear skies and a bright sun, and the weathervane's shadow is clearly visible as it reaches the beer keg. Floyd notes the shadow, makes a final check of the roasting pig, refills his plastic cup, wipes beer foam from his whiskers and positions himself in the tractor seat

"Who wants a hayride?" He shouts.

Jenny and I climb onto the hay wagon, seat ourselves on a straw bale, and wait for the other passengers to board. With everyone seated, Floyd starts the tractor and pulls the wagon away from the barn.

One of the passengers points out the fact that Nature seems to change moods with the seasons, and she is right. With winter approaching, the Brenner farm seems depressed. Most of the orange pumpkins have become Halloween decorations and the few that remain look lonely and abandoned.

Jenny notes the freshly cut corn stalks laying flat in the field and adds to the conversation.

"It looks like their waiting to be buried." She says. "And look at the sunflowers." They have their heads lowered. The farm looks sad."

Floyd is in a good mood and doesn't seem to notice. When the wagon is beyond the cornfield, he turns around in the tractor seat and, in a loud voice, begins narrating like a tour guide. He describes the Brenner farm in detail, letting the tractor lurch forward unguided, trusting it to follow the ruts and go where it should. Just beyond the sunflowers, the wagon rounds a patch of soybeans and the tree comes into view.

Anticipating a story, the hayride passengers become quiet. Floyd stops the tractor near the tree and turns off the noisy engine. With a dramatic flair, he takes one last sip of beer, places the empty plastic cup upside down on the tractor's shift handle, and points at the tree.

"It's been here longer than we know." Floyd begins. "According to legend the tree was here before the first Indians, and maybe before the first man, no one really knows. There used to be a riverbed here that channeled water from the melting glaciers up North. Before the river disappeared, this same tree stood at a point where two tributaries joined to form a larger river. According to Chippewa legend, when the white man arrived the river was almost gone. It was just a small creek, but the tree was there. The Chippewa thought the tree had magical properties and told stories, passed down from the people of the ice."

"When I was young," Floyd continued. "My grandfather told me the first Indians would bring offerings of freshly killed game to the tree, place the carcass over its low branches and let the tree's thorns suck the blood out of the dead animals leaving nothing behind but skin and bone."

Floyd's story was mesmerizing the hayride passengers and was scaring my daughter. She shivered, and put her hand on my arm.

"Yuk," she said, "Is any of this true?"

"I don't know," I answered. "I suppose it could be. I've heard of cave paintings of a tree with skins draped over its limbs."

Floyd finished his story, turned around in the tractor seat and started the engine. The puffing motor brought us back to reality, and back to our bouncy ride. Jenny kept her eyes on the tree as we headed back toward the barbeque. Jenny is smart, but she overcompensates for not having a mother and tries hard to behave like an adult. Attempting to make up for her earlier childish question, she turns toward me with a serious look.

"That was very interesting." She says.

I smiled and gave her a hug.

Back at the barn, with the tour over, Jenny finds a straw bale and makes herself' comfortable. Warmed by the sun, she drifts off to sleep. I chat with other guests and sample some of Grandma's potato salad.

Floyd notices the weathervanes shadow touching the barbeque and knowing the roasting pig is fully cooked, pounds a ladle against the metal frame holding the beer keg.

"Pig's ready, anybody hungry?"

Startled by the clang of a ladle, Jenny sits up brushing straw from her hair.

"Are you hungry?" I ask.

"No." she answers emphatically, "I had a nightmare about Floyd's tree!"

Worried the dream might have upset her; I ask if she wanted to tell me about it.

"Not now, maybe later, it was weird."

Jenny stays by my side for the rest of the afternoon. Floyd's guests share information and listen to stories about the farm. When the sun begins to set, the party ends, and everyone returns to their routines.

Jenny goes back to school, I go back to practicing law, Floyd and his father resume their exhausting schedule, and the tree waits.

CHAPTER TWO

A few weeks after the pig roast, Floyd's grandmother suffers a mild stroke. She remains mobile but needs help with heavy chores and Floyd decides to move into the old farmhouse to help her. Floyd has lived with his parents much too long and the old farmhouse is near the barn. If he stays with Grandma, his Father can drive home in the evening and pick him up for construction work in the morning. The move will save Floyd the drive to his father's house on the other side of the farm twice a day and give him more time to tend the cattle and help grandma.

Floyd loves his grandmother and, at first, they get along well. She is lonely and Floyd needs more separation from his parents. At first, the new living arrangement works well. Grandma and Floyd are comfortable and enjoy each other's company... until Floyd gets the piano.

Floyd had built a masonry fireplace for a friend who was unable to pay for the work. In lieu of payment, Floyd accepts an old grand piano. The piano has a broken leg, but is otherwise functional and Floyd sees the trade as an opportunity. He repairs the piano and has it tuned.

Floyd knows nothing about music, but now, he owns a piano. He uses the sheet music he finds in the piano bench and, on his own, learns to read music. He plinks out notes one at a time as he figures out where they go on the key board. It isn't music and listening to him as he strikes a key and then hesitates while he finds the next note, is maddening. He can only practice at night and it drives Grandma crazy. She threatens to burn the piano while Floyd was at work, but Floyd persists. He plinks out one note at a time until he is able to play with his right hand, then, one note at a time; he begins to train the left.

The piano gives Floyd an outside interest he desperately needs. His self-esteem improves and whenever I see him, he brags about the piano and gives me a progress report.

Late in November, snow comes to Ohio and new home construction slows. With less masonry work, Floyd finishes his farm chores early and spends more time on the keyboard. He is now playing what sounds like music and Grandma is a bit more tolerant, but she wishes he would stop playing the same piece, over and over.

Just before Thanksgiving, I stop at a small restaurant in town and find Floyd enjoying a cup of coffee. Floyd motions me to the stool next to him.

"I'm glad you stopped by", Floyd begins; I've been working on my music. Could you come to Grandma's house tonight to hear me play?"

Floyd was obviously proud of his musical accomplishments and I couldn't refuse. I didn't expect much. Floyd's hands were those of a farmer not of a musician. Having watched my daughter's small fingers during her piano lessons, I couldn't imagine Floyd being able to do much except poke at the keyboard one finger at a time. The possibility that Floyd's recital might be a disaster made me nervous, and thinking that Jenny's presence might mitigate what could be an embarrassing situation, I asked Floyd if my daughter could come with me. Floyd agreed, and a time was set for us to arrive.

CHAPTER THREE

Snow made the roads slippery as Jenny and I drove to the Brenner farm for the recital. I continued to worry about the outcome of Floyd's attempt to play the piano and counseled Jenny on a proper response if Floyd made a fool of himself.

"You know how hard it is to learn to play the piano." I began, "and you have a teacher!"

"Floyd has tried to teach himself and he might have gotten things wrong. If you made a lot of mistakes and I laughed at you, how would you feel?"

"Oh Dad!" Jenny responded. "I'm not going to laugh, and I make lots of mistakes. If you want to laugh at my mistakes I'm not going to cry or run away from home."

Jenny stared at the snow for a couple miles and then turned toward me.

"What are you going to do if Floyd screws up, clap and cheer?"

"No." I answered. I'm just going to try and be polite."

"Good luck with that." Jenny muttered.

When we arrived, Floyd and his father were just finishing their farm chores and I had a chance to chat with the older Brenner before he left for the new house on the other side of the farm. Floyd's father saw the snow as an opportunity. He liked to ride the snowmobile, and if he used the snowmobile to cut across the farm, rather than drive the truck home, Floyd could use the truck the next morning for any errands Grandma might have and wouldn't have to take his father to the other side of the farm and then come back for the recital. Floyd's father promised to be careful. Floyd protested, but after a short discussion, reluctantly agreed.

Floyd watched apprehensively as his father disappeared into the falling snow and after a few worried glances over his shoulder, led Jenny and me into the old farmhouse.

Before Floyd began his recital, Jenny played a simple piece she had memorized for her next lesson. I was proud of my daughter but worried that even her hesitant playing might shame the self-taught musician. When it was Floyd's turn, he placed a few pages of sheet music on the piano and seated himself on the old piano bench. Floyd's hands seemed even larger than I remembered and the music looked complicated. I held my breath as he put his huge hands on the keyboard.

I was wrong.

It wasn't perfect, but it was beautiful. The tempo was a bit off but I recognized it immediately as Chopin. How was it possible that this clumsy, mitt fisted, giant of a man, could play a complex piece of classical music without years of instruction?

Our discussion on the way to the Brenner farm about being polite now seemed ridiculous. Instead of avoiding an embarrassing moment, we now needed to respond appropriately to the unbelievable music coming from the old piano.

Floyd's large fingers moved gracefully over the keyboard as he peered intently at the sheet music. He had to stop occasionally to turn a page but he played beautifully. When he turned the last page, he stopped abruptly.

"That's all I've worked out." He said.

"My God," I responded, "That was beautiful. I knew you were an artist with stone and brick but that was unbelievable. Has your dad heard you play?

"No," Floyd answered, "I'm saving it for a Christmas surprise. I just hope I can learn the rest of it in time."

Jenny and I stayed long enough for a cup of hot chocolate and than drove home in the snow. The storm continued throughout the night, and roads and driveways needed plowed and shoveled the next morning.

It was late in the afternoon when one of Floyd's contractor friends called and gave me the bad news.

"Floyd's father was killed last night." The contractor began. "They just found his body impaled on that damn tree."

I assumed the accident had happened as the elder Brenner was coming back to get Floyd in the morning but I was wrong. The contractor set me straight.

"Floyd's mother thought her husband had stayed at Grandma's house because of the snow," he continued, "but when she called this morning and he wasn't there, they knew something was wrong."

"Who found him?" I asked.

The contractor continued.

"Floyd went out looking for him and found him stuck through the chest hanging off a limb in that same tree Floyd tells all the stories about. Floyd has gone a bit crazy and I'm on my way to see him."

"Can I help?" I asked.

"Not now," He responded, "but he wanted me to tell you something about his father not being able to hear him play at Christmas. Do you have any idea what he's talking about?"

I assured the contractor I understood and offered again to help. I didn't hear anything more until I was asked to attend the funeral.

CHAPTER FOUR

At the funeral home, Floyd sat up front, near his father's casket. His once friendly eyes were empty. He shook my hand but didn't seem to recognize me and didn't speak. Jenny accompanied me to the funeral and after viewing the body, asked me if the tree had killed Floyd's father, and if a tree could be evil. I told her it was just an accident, but secretly I had my doubts. The tree was much too peculiar, much too strange, and I wondered if a tree expert had ever looked at it to see what kind of tree it was.

After the funeral, some of us gave tribute to the elder Brenner by telling an anecdotal story. I offered a story about the barn.

I began by telling those attending the funeral that I had heard him refer to their barn as a bank barn quite often.

"I assumed the term was used because the barn held much of the farm's assets." I said. "But when I mentioned this to Floyd's Father at one of Floyd's roasts, he laughed and took the time to explain."

"The Barn," he said, "is a split-level structure with a hayloft above, a middle platform, and bullpens below. The long dirt ramp in front, leading up to the barn doors, is used to get machinery, straw and feed up to the middle platform where we can toss it down to the animals in the lower pens. The dirt ramp is a bank of dirt and that is where the barn gets its name. The barn is named after dirt, not money. We don't keep any money in the barn."

The funeral attendees laughed and Floyd perked up a bit. He shook my hand again as Jenny and I left. I promised to check on him but I didn't see him for weeks. Occasionally I would run into one of his friends who kept me informed as to his well-being. They were worried. Floyd didn't seem to be returning to his happy go lucky self. He became sullen and angry, got into a fight with one of his neighbors, and was nearly arrested.

Winter ran its course, warm weather returned and new homes were being built, but I didn't see Floyd on any construction sites. I worried that he might have given up the masonry business and I wanted to talk to him. Driving past the Brenner farm on a Friday, I saw Floyd's truck parked on the barn's ramp and decided to stop.

Grandma was busy hanging out clothes when I pulled into the drive and as I stepped out of my car, she pointed at the barn.

"He's just not right since his father died," she called out, "he's just not right."

I walked up the dirt embankment to the barn's front doors and spotted Floyd trying to toss a bale of hay into one of the lower pens using only one arm. The other arm was in a sling.

"It looks like you could use some help."

Startled, Floyd spun around. His cheek was bruised and swollen and he moved as if his ribs were painful.

"What happened?" I asked. "God I hope you didn't get into another fight."

"Yep I did." Floyd answered. "But not with a neighbor. It was that damn bull over there."

He pointed at a big black bull with sawed off horns

"I named him Chopin after the music I found in the piano bench." Floyd said. "Before my father was killed I could touch him without worrying about being kicked. After my Dad died Chopin became skittish and wouldn't let me pat him."

"He usually doesn't bother me when I go into the pen with him," Floyd continued, "but he's gotten mean lately. I turned my back and he charged me. He tossed me almost out of the pen but I hit the top rail and it broke my arm. I fell back in and he got me a couple more times He knocked out some of my teeth and broke my ribs. He threw me against the back of the pen so hard that it broke off a piece of timber and I managed to get a hold of it. I wacked him in the head and it stopped him just long enough for me to climb out. Chopin used to be my friend but ever since Dad died he doesn't like me."

"You're lucky to be alive," I responded, "I guess you won't be playing the piano for a while."

"A good long while," Floyd pointed at a pile of wood, wires, and white and black keys laying in the yard "If Dad can't hear me play nobody will. I beat the piano to death with a sledge hammer."

"What were you doing in the pen with a dangerous animal?" I asked.

"Sometimes I pen Chopin for breeding or medical attention." Floyd explained. "His strange behavior made me think he might be sick so I isolated him for a vet check. Usually I clean the pens before I let a bull in, but only one corner of Chopin's pen needed cleaning and I let him in before I started shoveling,"

"At first, Chopin stayed in the far end of the pen while I cleared the messy corner, but he was nervous. I saw him shaking his head and rubbing his horns on the post next to the pen door. I should have gotten out but I couldn't get images of the tree and of my father impaled on that damn limb out of my head. I knew it wasn't safe. Maybe I was having a death wish."

"I don't think so." I interrupted. "You fought back and you're here."

"Maybe." Floyd responded. "When I heard his hooves pounding, I turned just in time to see him coming directly at me with his head down. Chopin was ready to crush me against the pen's rails. He wanted to kill me."

"You took a hell of a beating." I interjected. "Are you going to get rid of the bull?"

"No. It was a fair fight and I deserved it. I was stupid when I let Dad take the snowmobile and I was stupid when I got into the pen with Chopin.

"From the look of you the bull won." I said.

"It was a hell of a fight." Floyd responded. "Chopin kept his head down and pawed at the floor, blowing dust with each snort. He caught me under my left arm and tossed me into the air like a toy. I landed on my back and was slow to get up. He hit me a couple more times before I got out."

After we finished our conversation, I said goodbye and walked past the remains of his piano on my way back to my car. It was obvious that the creative side of Floyd was gone. His father's death had turned him from a gentle giant into an angry farmer, and it was a shame. Before his father's accident, Floyd would design beautiful fireplaces by brushing sawdust off the plywood subfloor of a home under construction, and sketch out a half scale drawing of a finished fireplace. On his hands and knees, with only a square carpenter's pencil, he would draw an elaborate and wonderfully detailed picture of a fireplace, and then he would build it. Homeowners and builders all marveled at his talent and talked about it at every pig roast.

As I drove away, I noticed Floyd's minister pulling into the driveway. I was thankful others were trying to help and hoped the minister could convince Floyd that his anger was misplaced.

CHAPTER FIVE

After saying hello, Floyd and his minister went to the barn for a private talk, away from grandma's frequent interruptions. Floyd insisted the tree was evil, possessed, and that it had intentionally killed his father.

"I never trusted the damn tree," Floyd told his minister. "But because of the stories, my Dad never cut it down. Now, he's dead and who knows how many others might get hurt, or killed."

Floyd's Minister quoted Bible verses to assure Floyd that a tree was a passive instrument of God, and that even death was part of God's greater plan.

Floyd wasn't buying it.

"So why couldn't the tree be like the burning bush in reverse?" Floyd asked. "If God can appear to man in the form of a bush, why can't the Devil appear in the form of a tree? The Bible talks about the tree of knowledge in the Garden of Eden having bad fruit so who is to say my damn tree isn't just as bad?"

Surprised by Floyd's question the minister stood silent for a moment before answering.

"I don't believe the Devil is capable of a modern day appearance, but why don't we put your fears to rest by going to the tree and pray."

At first, Floyd refused. He hated the tree and, after his father's death, he had avoided it. He even suspected that it had somehow infected his bull with an evil spirit and caused Chopin to attack him.

Eventually the minister convinced Floyd to face his fears and they began their walk to the tree. They passed new corn sprouting randomly in the unplanted field and passed the empty pumpkin patch. Except for the cattle, the farm appeared neglected and would soon become unprofitable. Taxes and feed bills had to be paid and, if the neglect continued, the farm could fall into arrears.

"You know," The minister offered. "If the farm lays fallow for too long it will create debts you can't cover. You need to continue in the family tradition and keep it profitable."

Floyd was indifferent.

"Grandma is almost eighty," Floyd answered. "She will be gone soon and only my mother and I will be left. It all seems pointless. Let the tree have the farm if it wants it. It's been here a lot longer than we have."

For Floyd the tree was an evil presence and now it was asserting its dominance. Floyd wanted no part of it, but out of respected for his minister, he followed him meekly to the tree.

When they reached the spot where Floyd's father had died, the minister stood close to the tree and, unknowingly, stood directly under the broken limb that had impaled Floyd's father. Floyd stood back. The tree brought back horrible memories. His skin turned cold and his mind filled with ugly images.

He could see his father on the snowmobile, squinting to see through the falling snow. Having ridden the snowmobile often, Floyd knew the snowmobile's headlights reflected off the snowflakes, making it almost impossible to see ahead. Floyd imagined his father cursing the snow and twisting the throttle in anger to pick up speed wanting to get home before the snow got worse. He imagined the roots of the tree responding to the approaching snowmobile, pulling up and out of the earth in small loops becoming snares for an unsuspecting pray.

In Floyd's mind, he could see the ski of the snowmobile catch in the waiting trap. He could see the ski snap and the snowmobile twist violently. He could see the rear of the snowmobile kick up and toss his father into the air and onto the jagged limb. He could see his father try to free himself and then give up as death swept over him.

The images were too much for Floyd. He sank to his knees, sobbing. The minister took Floyd's collapse as a sign of God's presence and began to pray.

"God give this man the vision to see the truth, the wisdom to understand your purpose, and the strength to endure the loss of his father. Give him the ability to see this tree as only an innocent plant, one of your wonderful creations, put here to serve man, not to cause injury or harm. Let the anger and pain leave your servant and be replaced with your grace and soothing presence."

As he began his final words, the minister placed his hand on the tree just below the jagged limb where a small amount of milky sap was exposed.

"This we ask in the name of our savior....." He touched the tree to give it his blessing and the tree sap instantly burned his hand.

"JESUS CHRIST!" he shouted, "The son of a bitch just bit me.

CHAPTER SIX

Summer passed and hunting season arrived. Floyd and his father often hunted deer together and out of habit, or maybe remorse, Floyd dug out his deer rifle and hiked out toward the pumpkin patch. He had just passed the empty cornfield when he spotted a doe with two young fawn standing between him and the evil tree. He would normally never consider shooting a doe, especially one with fawns, but the tree had sucked the soul out of him. He raised his rifle and was about to pull the trigger when he realized what he was doing. He wasn't hunting. He was killing. The revelation made him realize that the tree wasn't the only monster on the Brenner farm.

"What am I doing," he muttered, "What have I become?"

He lowered his rifle, tipped his head back and screamed an anguished guttural scream and everything went blank.

***

Floyd was in a semi-conscious state when the ambulance reached the hospital. Police were waiting in case he became violent, but the precaution was unnecessary. Floyd had been sedated in the ambulance and remained quiet. He was confused, in pain, and drifted in and out of consciousness. His vital signs were taken while nurses tried to trim away a sticky substance in his beard without touching the blisters underneath. They tried to wash the stuff off his hands and beard but couldn't. The milky substance was definitely not water-soluble and it was turning reddish brown as it absorbed blood and body fluids through Floyd's skin.

When the emergency room doctor arrived, he recognized Floyd. He and his two sons had been guests at many of Floyd's pig roasts. Floyd's eyes were wild and he was pulling at his restraints. The patient strapped to the gurney was a transfigured version of the jovial host the Doctor remembered. The patient on the gurney was disfigured, in pain, and needed help.

When the doctor bent over Floyd, he was repulsed by the stink of the strange sticky substance on Floyd's beard. It was obvious that the left side of Floyd's face was being dissolved.

"Whatever that stuff is we need to get it off and we need to get it off fast."

"We tried water but it didn't help," replied one of the nurses, "His skin is blistered and I'm afraid to try alcohol."

"Try lard on some of the hair you've already cut off," the Doctor directed. "It looks like an acid gum. Call the cafeteria and have them bring up a can of Crisco."

Floyd calmed down as a second dose of pain medication took effect and stopped thrashing against his restraints.

"What happened?" Floyd asked.

"You're in the hospital." The Doctor replied. "You have a substance on your face and hands that is blistering your skin. Do you know what it is?"

Floyd tried to remember, but had only a fuzzy recollection of a deer running toward a tree.

"I don't know." He answered. "I don't know."

"It looks like milkweed sap but less viscous. Could it be from a plant? I've treated thistle burns and poison ivy but nothing this powerful. How long has this stuff been on your skin?"

"I don't know," answered Floyd. "I only remember the ambulance." Floyd closed his eyes, exhausted.

The Crisco proved effective in dissolving the goo and seemed to stop the blistering.

One of the nurses complimented the doctor.

"Good call Doc."

"Not good medicine," Replied the doctor. "It was a guess. When I was a kid, a bully put chewing gum in my hair and a local baker used lard to dissolve it.

"Whatever works." replied the nurse.

With Floyd's wounds cleaned and his beard removed, his injuries were re-examined. The burns on his face were deep and would be disfiguring. The burns on his hands were also deep and might result in some loss of function. His face would require plastic surgery to replace lost flesh and until then, Floyd would probably want to keep the left side of his face covered.

I was in my law office when I found out that Floyd was in the hospital. One of his neighbors called me.

"Floyd has been taken to the hospital," he said, "I don't know much, but after seeing police cars near Floyd's barn I thought he might need a lawyer."

I thanked the neighbor for calling and rushed to the hospital. After making several inquiries, the receptionist sent me to the emergency room where I found a police officer and a reporter waiting outside the emergency room door.

I told the officer I was Floyd's lawyer, and asked what was going on. Instead of a civil answer, he put me off by claiming he wasn't at liberty to say.

The reporter was a bit more cooperative. "Are you here to see Floyd?" she asked.

"Yes I am. I'm Floyd's lawyer. I was told that Floyd was brought here after a police presence at his farm. Do you know what this is all about?"

The reporter introduced herself as Daphne, a reporter for the local Gazette.

"I know a little," she said, "but not everything. He has some sort of burns and was acting very strange when they brought him in."

I wasn't getting very far with either the police officer or the reporter so I stepped around them and looked through a small window in the emergency room door. I recognized the Doctor as a regular guest at Floyd's pig roasts and tapped on the glass to get his attention. One of the nurses came to the door.

"Can I help you?" The nurse asked.

"I'm Floyd's attorney and as soon as possible I need to talk to him."

Floyd hadn't retained me but I assumed he would need council and after the report of police at the Brenner Farm, the sooner he was represented the better. Until Floyd could make a choice, I was volunteering.

While I waited, Daphne introduced herself more formally. She explained her position with the newspaper and asked to accompany me when I talked to Floyd. At first, I refused. I had seen Daphne before on a few occasions but didn't want to bring the media into a lawyer client conversation.

Daphne was attractive, about Floyd's age, well dressed, well spoken, and not in the least hesitant about repeating her request.

"I was on the scene just after the Sheriff arrived," she volunteered, "and I can probably fill you in on a few more details. If I come in with you I may also be able to point out things that will help you ask important questions."

She had a point. So far, I was completely in the dark.

"OK," I said, "You can come with me, but just listen."

When Floyd regained full consciousness, he realized he was handcuffed to his bed and that his face and hands were bandaged. He was confused and didn't like being restrained. The Doctor was reluctant to allow any visitors but eventually relented when I stressed the importance of Floyd having legal council as soon as possible. I explained

Daphne's position, and we entered the emergency room together.

At first, we stood beside Floyd's bed in silence. I had no idea what had caused Floyd to be in such a predicament. He had been through hell lately, and had just recovered from the injuries Chopin, the bull, had inflicted. Now, he had been burned and was handcuffed to a hospital bed. I assumed he had attempted suicide.

I tried to question him but he didn't answer. He was frightened and could only see half the room because of the bandages on the left side of his face.

After several attempts to clear his throat, Floyd managed to speak.

"What's going on?"

"Where am I?"

"Thank God you're awake." I responded. "You've been drifting in and out of consciousness and I need your help to get your handcuffs off. Do you remember what happened?"

"No." answered Floyd, "What's wrong with my hands and why is my head bandaged?"

"The Doctor says you were burned by a sticky substance that caused your skin and flesh to blister. Luckily, the Doctor neutralized it before it could do any more damage. They're still analyzing the stuff but they don't have any answers yet. Can you remember how it got on your skin?

"No." Floyd answered in an angry voice. "No, I don't remember! Get me out of here!"

Floyd began yanking on the handcuffs, banging them against the bed rail. The Doctor's voice came from the back of the room urging Floyd to calm down and admonishing me for aggravating his patient.

"That's enough," He said, "Floyd obviously can't remember, and until he is completely lucid you will have to figure out what happened on your own. You need to leave now!"

"Is that you doc?" Floyd asked, trying to turn his head far enough to see beyond his bandages.

"Yes Floyd, it's me and you're going to be ok."

The Doctor repeated his command for Daphne and me to leave and politely ushered us to the door.

As I stepped out of the room, I had to maneuver around the officer stationed in the hallway. I assumed he was part of a suicide watch but when Daphne and I walked by he stood up and addressed me in a commanding voice.

"So, is he finally awake? We need to question him and I'm tired of setting here. The sooner he can be moved to the jail the better."

I stopped and turned toward the officer. His remarks were uncalled for and raised more questions. Why would the police be taking a suicidal individual to jail?

I answered the officer's question with an abrupt and angry voice.

"I'm Mr. Brenner's lawyer and no one questions him unless I am present, and not until he is ready to be questioned. There is an injured man, handcuffed to a hospital bed in that room for no reason. We all want to know what happened and your job is to keep people out, not play detective. He has been through hell and we need to keep him safe until he recovers. If you've got pressing personal issues you should ask to be replaced."

I was about to lay into the officer again, when Daphne pulled me away. She suggested we go to the hospital cafeteria for coffee.

"For a minuet I thought you were going to hit the cop." Daphne said with a smile.

"I damn near did. How did everyone get the idea there was a crime committed, and how did this get to be newsworthy enough to draw you in?"

As we walked to the cafeteria, Daphne explained her position.

"I can probably answer some of your questions but a lot of people are making unwarranted assumptions and both of us are going to have our hands full getting at the truth, you as an attorney and me as a journalist."

After filling our coffee cups in the hospital cafeteria line, and discarding several dirty spoons from the spoon holder, Daphne found a table in a far corner and we sat down to talk. As I stirred cream into my coffee, Daphne broke the silence.

"After seeing all those dirty spoons I think I'll drink mine black."

I grinned and put my used spoon on the table directly in front of Daphne to annoy her. She covered it with her napkin.

"The truth of all this is like that spoon," I pointed out. "You're a reporter and I'm a lawyer and no matter how dirty the spoon, we can't afford to cover it up."

I removed the napkin.

"You're right," Answered Daphne, "There are already too many assumptions and before Floyd gets railroaded by an ambitious prosecutor or a runaway press we need to know the truth and he needs to know the truth even more than we do. Does he know that his grandmother is dead?"

"Hell No!" I answered. "I didn't know that! When did this happen? There is obviously a great deal you know that I don't and I need to be brought up to speed, now!"

I pointed at Daphne and spoke in a commanding voice.

"Tell me everything you know!"

"Don't get angry," She said. "I thought you knew or I would have told you sooner."

"Well, tell me now!"

44

"I picked up on the story earlier today," Daphne began, "when the Gazette monitored a nine-one-one call from Floyd saying a tree had killed his grandmother. I got the location from the police dispatcher and arrived shortly after the cops. Because of the weird call, and the bizarre scene I knew it was more than a local farm accident so I called my old boss."

"I work for the local news paper now, but two years ago I worked for Channel Three. My old boss agreed the story had legs and sent their helicopter. Things escalated from there."

She took a sip of coffee and continued.

"I interviewed the deputy that arrived first and he told me he found Floyd near the barn, standing over an old women's lifeless body making howling sounds and pulling at his beard. He told me the sight of a screaming giant trying to rip his face off while standing over a dead or unconscious old women, prompted him to park at a safe distance and wait for backup.

I noticed a pile of meat chunks and blood near the old woman. The scene was so bizarre we both stayed in our cars until back up arrived. Two other Sheriff's cars arrived next, and while the Sheriff was deciding on a plan of action, Floyd collapsed. A deputy approached and prodded Floyd with his foot and got no response. He told me later that there was stuff on Floyd's face that looked like it had melted half his beard and some of his flesh and that it smelled awful."

After another sip of coffee, Daphne continued her story.

"When things seemed safe I got out of my car and got the Sheriff to talk to me. He told me he checked the old woman and found her dead and before I could get any more out of him an ambulance arrived. Floyd was strapped to a stretcher and with the attendants obviously avoiding the goo on his hands and face, loaded him onto the ambulance, and, with windows open to clear the stench, took off for the nearest hospital.

I shook my head in disbelief. "Is there anything else?"

"Yes there is she replied."

"The Channel Three helicopter took less than twenty minuets to arrive and I directed it to land in a nearby field. I gave the crew a quick overview and briefed the TV station manager by radio. He asked me to cover the story and instructed the crew of the chopper to set up a live feed."

"As soon as the camera was active I gave my initial report. When I signed off, I tried to get close to the other emergency vehicle while the old woman's body was being loaded, but I was pushed away and almost stepped into the pool of blood and meet chunks. The police cars and the helicopter began to attract passers-by and a traffic jam developed in front of the farm. When the road became blocked, the Sheriff and his deputies were forced to leave the crime scene and direct traffic. The Sheriff called the State police for assistance and after a few minuets, more police cars showed up. With so many flashing lights the farm took on the appearance of a disaster scene and I was quick to capitalize on the situation."

"I ordered the news chopper airborne and instructed them to film the confusion. As a result, what should have remained a local story instantly went viral. When I got back to my desk at the Gazette my editor made a call to Channel Three and arranged for me to cover the story for the TV station as well as the newspaper, and now it looks like I'm obligated to you and this damn spoon as well."

"Yes you are," I answered, "and I want you to put that spoon in your purse and keep it there as a reminder of that obligation until this is over."

CHAPTER SEVEN

My first priority was to get Floyd's handcuffs removed, but I had no information about the cause of his grandmother's death or about the events that resulted in his burns. I had nothing to argue with, nothing to convince the police or the prosecutor that he was safe to release him. His psychotic break was apparently real, and considering what he had been through, understandable. His father was dead, his favorite bull had attacked him, and now his grandmother was dead.

My first stop was to see the County Sheriff. I hoped he would be cooperative. I needed answers, and for Floyd's sake, I needed them quickly. When Floyd's hospital stay ended, he would be put in jail unless I could make sense out of a series of very strange events.

The sheriff's office was crowded when I arrived and it took a moment to get past the desk officer. Luckily, the Sheriff recognized me and motioned me into his office.

"I am representing Floyd Butler," I explained, "and need information. I especially need to know what crime Floyd is suspected of committing and if charges have been filed."

"I don't know much more than you do." The Sheriff responded. "I do think the prosecutor will press charges and I'm looking for answers just like you are. I'm headed to the Brenner farm as soon as I finish with this paper work."

The Sheriff pointed at a folder on his desk.

"Why don't you meet me at the farm and we can share what little we do know?"

The Sheriff arrived at the farm first. He was busy replacing yellow crime scene tape when I pulled into the driveway.

"Damn," the Sheriff said, "I can't afford to keep a deputy out here to keep this from happening and whoever is snooping around is not only contaminating a crime scene but possibly stealing stuff."

"Why not get someone you trust to stay out here in a travel trailer and provide twenty four hour coverage until you can take the tape down?"

"Good idea," Replied the Sheriff. "I may be able to get the county to cough up a small stipend to make their stay worthwhile, and Floyd's mother may want them to perform some farm chores."

I agreed to help follow up on the idea while the sheriff led me to a burned spot in the grass left over from Floyd's recent barbeque. Bloodstains were evident in the grass nearby.

"We found a mutilated fawn here, and I mean mutilated." The sheriff pointed at the bloody grass. "It looked like someone had taken a chain saw to it. We found the old woman over there, laying on her back with Floyd standing over her. He was screaming and ripping at his beard. Thankfully, he collapsed before we had to use force. I checked the old woman for a pulse but she was gone. There were no obvious marks on her to indicate a cause of death and I couldn't tell if she had been moved. We called for an ambulance and before we could do much else the press arrived, a helicopter landed, and a traffic jamb developed that took us away from the crime scene. We only got things under control after the State Police got here to help. With them directing traffic we were able to expand our investigation in this direction."

The Sheriff began walking toward the cornfield as he continued his account.

"We searched the barn and the house and didn't find anything unusual, but one of my deputies found a blood trail leading this way."

The sheriff pointed toward the tree in the distance. When we reached the tree, the stench was overwhelming. A deer carcass with a badly broken leg lay under the tree.

"This is what we found, along with that chain saw."

The Sheriff pointed at a chain saw stuck almost half way through the tree's trunk.

"Does this make any sense to you?" I asked. "Did the broken leg bring that deer down?"

"Maybe." answered the Sheriff, "but a rifle was over there, next to the blood trail that leads back to the barn. It was empty and there are bullet holes in the tree."

We walked back to the barn and sat in the Sheriff's car to continue our conversation.

"What else can you tell me?" I asked.

"Not much," answered the Sheriff, "except that there was blood and shredded meat on Floyd's clothing and dried blood on the chain saw stuck in the tree. There was also a little bit of the goo that was in Floyd's beard on grandma's clothing."

I continued to question the Sheriff. "Have you put together a scenario for all of this that might make sense?"

"Not really." The sheriff answered.

He rubbed his hands together and stared through the police car's windshield at the spot where they had found Floyd's grandmother.

"I'm waiting on lab results from the blood samples we took from Floyd's clothing and off the saw. We're also waiting on the autopsy report. At this point we don't even know what caused the woman to die, but with all the blood, and Floyd's erratic behavior, I thought it was best to hold Floyd on suspicion."

The Sheriff turned toward me.

"You were friends with Floyd, what can you tell me about him as a person?"

I answered as truthfully as I could. The Sheriff had been forthcoming with me and I felt a responsibility to reciprocate.

"I met with Floyd's father to discuss tax matters more than I interacted with Floyd. I've seen Floyd at his best and at his worst, and there are stories about that tree that might surprise you."

We continued our conversation for nearly an hour. I described Floyd's fascination with the tree, his artistic abilities, his piano experience, and his battle with Chopin the bull. I also described the depression brought on by his father's death. I gave an overall assessment of Floyd as a gentle man incapable of intentionally harming anyone. I agreed with the Sheriff that it was impossible to draw any firm conclusions until we had more facts.

"There are no witnesses." The Sheriff continued. "Only Floyd knows what actually happened and unless he regains his memory, we have to depend on secondary evidence, evidence that is very confusing. We know nothing about what might have happened earlier in the day his grandmother died, or if Floyd and his grandmother were getting along or if they had argued."

"From the scant evidence available," The Sheriff observed. "We only know that a strange series of events occurred over a relatively short span of time. We can't be certain when the events began or in what order they took place. We only knew when they ended."

I had a scheduled court appearance on an unrelated matter that afternoon and tried to see the County Prosecutor while I was near his office.

Unfortunately, he was unavailable but I did learn that an arraignment hearing had been scheduled for Thursday. That gave me just two days to complete my investigation. I returned to my office to try to make sense out of what little I knew.

Floyd could give me everything I needed if his memory returned and it was important for me to be there if that happened, but that seemed impossible.

I called Daphne to solicit her help.

"Daphne, this is Floyd's lawyer. I have only two days to prepare for Floyd's arraignment and I've got very little to go on. I need to keep investigating but I also need to know if Floyd starts to remember anything. Can you check on him from time to time and let me know if his memory starts to return?"

"My boss wants me to stay on the story." Daphne responded, "Continuing to interview Floyd is one way to do that, so sure, I would be happy to keep an eye on him."

Daphne returned to the hospital to find Floyd in a private room. After verifying that she was working with me, she was admitted to his room. She found Floyd resting comfortably but still handcuffed to the bed rails.

The large bandages on his face and hands had been replaced with smaller wrappings, and a bit more of his face was exposed. His appearance wasn't as shocking as it had been immediately after his admittance, but seeing such a strong and vibrant man confined, helpless, and possibly scarred for life, was difficult for Daphne.

"Is he coherent?" Daphne asked the nurse.

"Yes," the nurse answered in a whisper, "but he still doesn't remember much. He remembers things before the incident but nothing about getting burned and he still hasn't been told about his grandmother, so please be careful."

Daphne walked to Floyd's bedside and put her hand on his arm. She spoke in a soft voice.

"Are you awake?"

Floyd turned his head toward her.

"How are you feeling?" Daphne asked. "Are you still in pain?"

"A little bit." Floyd replied. "Did you come to take me home?

There was such sadness and desperation in Floyd's voice that Daphne had to fight back tears.

"No, not yet," she answered, "when you are better and your burns are healed, then you can go home."

Daphne knew she was making promises she couldn't keep but she felt compelled to offer comfort. Floyd's question about going home also made her realize that when he was released he would probably have no home and no life to return to. Floyd had been cast adrift by circumstances that he couldn't control, and couldn't remember, and he was asking her questions she couldn't, or wasn't allowed to answer. Daphne left Floyd's hospital room firmly committed to finding the truth.

CHAPTER EIGHT

Daphne arrived at my office to report on her hospital visit just as I was about to sequester myself in an attempt to put some order to the strange events. I invited Daphne into my conference room, told my secretary to hold my calls, and motioned Daphne to a seat.

Daphne was wearing an especially attractive dress that complimented her blonde hair. Until now, I hadn't taken notice of how attractive she was, but her blue eyes and smile suddenly got my attention. She was beautiful, smart and single but I was at least ten years her senior and had a ten-year-old daughter. I was also single, but I had no right to be interested in someone so young. I tried to ignore her appearance but I was hypnotized by her allure.

Daphne noticed my long stare and quickly deflected my obvious distraction by insisting we get to the point of our meeting. I was embarrassed but regained my composure and focused my attention on the matter at hand.

"I'm trying to make sense of the few things we know about the events surrounding the death of Floyd's grandmother and I could use your help."

"Definitely," Daphne answered, "I want to help in any way I can."

I was glad I had brought her in. Having someone to help sort through the logical order of the events could prove valuable. Daphne suggested we list all the things we knew on three by five cards and put them in order. It seemed like a good idea but it wasn't easy. Listing the facts was simple, putting them in order wasn't.

Grandma had died, but we didn't even know the cause of her death. She could have died at the end of our list, while Floyd was standing over her, or at the beginning, or somewhere in between. The chainsaw was stuck in the tree in an obvious attempt to cut it down, most likely by Floyd, but when? A doe with a broken leg lay dead under the tree. Had it been shot, and did the dead doe have anything to do with the mutilated fawn found near the barn? There were bullets in the tree but no way to know when it had been shot. A hunting rifle was found about fifty feet from the tree next to a blood trail leading from the tree toward the barn, or the barn toward the tree, again there was no way to tell.

It seemed reasonable to assume that the rifle had been used by Floyd to shoot the tree, but again, we were working with assumptions. There was a mutilated fawn near the barn and near Grandma's body but not close enough for direct blood transfer from the fawn. There was also blood on the saw, on Floyd's clothing and on Grandma's clothing. Where the blood came from and how it got there were still unknowns.

Tree sap had probably burned Floyd's face and hands. There were also small amounts on Grandma's clothing, but none on the gun.

We wrote our facts on the three by five cards and moved them around on my desk to create several possible scenarios. None of the arrangements led us to a conclusion or to a definite chain of events. We assumed the fawn had been mutilated with the same chain saw that was stuck in the tree and assumed the fawn had to have been cut near the barn where it was found. It was far too mutilated to have been moved after being cut. The only chain saw found at the scene was now stuck in the tree, which indicated the fawn had been cut first, and the saw then taken to the tree where it was stuck. The blood found on the saw was probably from the fawn but until it was tested, we were guessing. Beyond our sequence related to the saw, any hope of coming up with a scenario that would explain everything, proved fruitless.

Daphne left with the excuse she had other errands. I continued to shuffle the cards but the more I tried the more I realized that forensic information was essential for me to make the pieces fit. My next stop was the Coroner's office.

The coroner was just finishing his examination of Floyd's grandmother when I interrupted him. At first, he was reluctant to share his results but after a call to the County Prosecutor he consented and let me listen to a recording of his observations.

"The elder Mrs. Brenner apparently died of a heart attack. What caused the heart attack is still in question. According to laboratory results, the blood on her clothing

*is the same blood found on the chain saw and on Floyd.
The blood is not human and it all came from the same
animal. The deceased had several broken ribs and it
is difficult to tell if the injuries occurred, pre, or post
mortem, they did, however, occur almost coincidently
with the heart attack. There was some bruising on her
chest that is either from trauma or from her laying face
down for a period of time just after death. According to
the observations of the first responder, the time of death
was probably no more than thirty minutes before the
police arrived. The deceased was suffering from arterial
sclerosis and osteoporosis and had suffered a recent
stroke. She also had several old stress fractures in her
arms and hands."*

I listened intently and one item in his report worried
me. I asked the Coroner for more information.

"Could the healed fractures indicate abuse?"

"Yes," the Coroner answered, "but they could also
be from other causes. Most were just hairline fractures
and could have resulted from her brittle bone condition
and normal activity."

After listening to the Coroner's report, I understand
the prosecutor's reasons for suspecting that a crime might

have been committed, and that sufficient circumstantial evidence might exist to charge Floyd with manslaughter, or murder. The Coroner's findings were potentially damning but could also be helpful if I could make the pieces fit. The possibility that Floyd might be falsely accused using only circumstantial evidence made me even more determined to uncover the missing facts.

From the Coroner's office I drove to the County Court House to see the Prosecutor and insisted that the supposed crime scene be better protected. The Prosecutor was courteous and let me into his office without an appointment.

After exchanging pleasantries, I explained that I had met with the Sheriff earlier at the Brenner farm.

"There has been some vandalism and a possible compromise of the supposed crime scene." I began.

"Neither of us are going to get at the facts unless the farm is better protected and the area of interest be expanded to include the tree and the blood trail between the tree and the area where the body was found. The Sheriff suggests a trusted individual camp out on the farm to protect the area from the curious and the press."

The prosecutor agreed.

"I'll go along with the idea of additional protection but only with an official presence, someone with authority and training."

"For me to prove Floyd guilty I need uncontaminated evidence just as you need it to prove Floyd innocent."

Our agreement was automatic and a temporary police presence was in place that afternoon.

I called Daphne as soon as I left the prosecutor's office. I needed to bring her up to speed on the Coroner's findings and I wanted to stay abreast of the attention the press was giving the story.

The latest headlines read,:

"Tree maims son and kills father and grandmother."

Daphne answered her phone promptly.

"Daphne, I'm worried about the way reporters have begun to focus on the tree as a way to get air time and column space. They are inventing wild stories and stressing its involvement in the death of both Grandma and Floyd's father. The tree is becoming tabloid fodder and it isn't doing Floyd's case any good."

Daphne agreed that we needed to deal in facts and sensationalism could only damage the case. We both also realized that our lives were being dominated by Floyd's dilemma. Maybe the myths about the tree were true. I had begun to believe some of them, and Daphne wanted to examine the mythical side of the story further.

Daphne knew my daughter was a fan of Floyd's stories and asked if she could talk to her. Other than Floyd, Jenny knew more about the legends surrounding the tree than anyone else. Unfortunately, she had created some of them herself.

I should have refused Daphne's request but it gave me another excuse to see her in a social setting. I agreed to let her talk to Jenny but to put it off until later.

Daphne talked to Floyd's Doctor about the nature of Floyd's burns and the substance found on his beard and hands. She was convinced that it was tree sap, and reasoned that if anyone else had been burned, it would provide confirmation that the tree was responsible. Floyd couldn't remember immediate events but if the tree had injured someone else, Floyd might remember it as an event before his memory loss.

To follow up on her hunch, Daphne returned to the hospital. At first, she concentrated on comforting Floyd, but as soon as she felt he was ready, she began to ask him direct questions.

"Floyd. Have you ever been burned before?"

"I burned my hand once on my barbeque." Floyd answered. "But not like this. Do you know what happened to me?"

"No I don't." Daphne answered. "Do you remember where you were when the stuff that burned you got on your skin?"

Floyd shook his head slowly and she could tell from his expression that he felt lost.

"Did anyone else ever get burned on your farm?" Daphne asked.

Floyd's answer surprised her.

"Yes, my minister burned his hand on the same tree that killed my Dad. I took him to the hospital just to make sure he was all right. Is that what burned me? Did that damn tree burn me?"

Floyd became excited and tried to sit up. Daphne backed away and gestured for him to calm down.

"I don't know," she said, "but I'll find out, I promise."

Daphne left Floyd's hospital room even more committed to finding the truth. With another recorded incident of a burn caused by the same tree, Daphne would have something more than speculation and the information she needed might be as close as the medical building next to the hospital. Patient privacy laws prevented her from searching through hospital records but a bizarre incident, like being burned by tree sap, should have been reported to the County Health Department, and most of its records were open public records.

The Department receptionist remembered the incident and made Daphne a sanitized copy of the report. Patient identification had been deleted but Floyd had already identified his minister and Daphne now had written confirmation of another burn caused by sap from the same tree.

She immediately called Floyd's minister.

"Reverend, this is Daphne with Channel Three News. Are you aware that Floyd Brenner is in the hospital with burns from the same tree that burned you?"

"No," Answered the reverend, "I heard he was in the hospital but I didn't know he was burned, how bad was he burned? I only touched a tiny bit of sap from the tree but now I have a permanent scar in the shape of the number seven on my left palm. Can he have visitors yet? Floyd was convinced that the tree was evil. Do you think it might be evil?"

"I don't know." Answered Daphne, "but I need your help to prove that the tree's history and peculiar nature are more than just a collection of myths."

"My religion allows for demons and evil spirits," replied the Minister. "Being possessed by an evil spirit has been evidenced in man and some animals, but other than the tree of knowledge, the tree of life and the burning bush I am not aware of possessed plants, and the ones in the Bible were possessed by God, not by evil."

Daphne dodged a lengthy religious discussion by asking another question.

"I appreciate your dilemma in explaining the tree in biblical terms but I am primarily interested in how you were burned, not why you touched the tree."

The minister gave Daphne a hesitant answer.

"I placed my hand on the tree to give it my blessing and touched a small amount of its sap. The sap stuck to my hand and burned me. I couldn't get it off so Floyd drove me to the hospital. They also had trouble getting the stuff off my hand and it left a scar, a scar in the shape of an evil symbol referred to in the bible. I may have been marked by the Devil and Floyd may be right about the tree being evil."

It wasn't the answer Daphne wanted, but she was happy with the additional information. The tree had actually burned someone else. The minister's story however would only add to the hysteria surrounding the tree if his religious interpretation became common knowledge. Daphne decided to wait before bringing him into the spotlight. She needed facts but the tree was surrounded by myths, myths that Floyd had kept alive, and had possibly created, myths that were now being solidified by the death of two people.

CHAPTER NINE

Daphne's immediate goal was to get more information on the tree. What kind of a tree was it, and why was there no more like it in the area? She started her search for an expert by contacting the director of the local Botanical Gardens. When she explained Floyd's burns and the possibility that they were the result of contact with tree sap, the Garden's director referred Daphne to a renowned dendrologist at Ohio State University. It took several attempts but Dr. Brice finally returned Daphne's call.

"Dr. Brice, I am a reporter working on an unusual case involving a tree. I have been told you may be the man that can identify the tree and explain its strange features."

"Woody plants, including trees, are my field, but we are still learning. What strange features are you concerned about?"

"The tree is growing on a farm in Northern Ohio," Daphne explained, "and aside from its strange appearance, there are mythical beliefs that it has been alive since the last ice age. It has a sap that causes burns when touched and two people have been burned recently, one seriously."

Dr. Brice gave Daphne a pedantic response typical of a university professor.

"There are a dozen or more poisonous trees, a few of which are quite dangerous, but none like what you are describing grow in the mid latitudes and none are indigenous to Ohio. The laburnum tree has never existed anywhere in the United States and you might want to look for another source for the burns."

Discouraged but not deterred, Daphne repeated the fact that two individuals had definitely been burned by the tree's sap, and one was still hospitalized.

"The press is using exaggerations and myths to make the tree into a monster and gain ratings. We desperately need a rational scientific explanation to counter the myths being propagated by the press."

"This is more than just a curious tree," Daphne continued, "there have been multiple deaths associated with the tree and there is an impending indictment of an individual for manslaughter that hangs on an accurate identification of the tree and its characteristics."

The scientist was put-off by the criminal aspect of the situation but took Daphne's request to combat myth with scientific knowledge as a personal challenge and agreed to examine the tree.

"I can try to get one of the University's airplanes and fly into a local airport this weekend. Would that meet your schedule?"

Daphne agreed and as soon as she hung up with Dr. Brice, she contacted me.

"I'm glad I caught you," she began, "I have an expert from Ohio State that is willing to look at the tree and I need to arrange for access this weekend."

The Sheriff gave his approval and Saturday morning, Daphne and I met Dr. Brice at the County Airport. As we drove to the Brenner farm, I gave the famous scientist a short rundown of the events that had put Floyd into the hospital and into handcuffs. By the time we arrived at the farm, Dr. Brice's interest had been peaked.

"What you are describing is a Hippomane Macinella," said Dr. Brice, "but they are only found in the sub tropics, Florida and the Caribbean. The entire tree is toxic and oozes sap when it rains that can blister the skin. Even raindrops running off its leaves can cause blisters and if it is burned the smoke is deadly. It also produces small green apples that are poisonous and, if eaten, can cause an agonizing death. The only other thing I can think of is a large bush found in the rainforest called Dendrocnide Moroides. The natives call it the stinging tree. It grows to over six feet tall and has stinging hairs like a nettle. A sting causes a swollen area covered by small red spots. A sting is very painful, can last for months, and occasionally can be fatal. The other possibility is a Milky Mangrove, a member of the Spurge family, which has a milky sap that can cause blistering, but it is found only in the tropics. One of the Milky Mangrove's cousins has small round nuts that the natives burn like candles. Your description of the exposed roots is not very typical in these plants however, and has me very curious."

When we reached the farm, I spoke to the guard on duty and we were allowed to proceed to the tree.

The dead doe still lay under the tree but it had been mummified. I pointed out the condition of the doe and described its smelly condition just a few days before.

"The ability of the tree's roots to suck fluids out of animals is one of the myths Floyd tells about the tree," I explained, "but with Floyd unable to tell all the stories there is only one person I can think of that has memorized most of them. Unfortunately, she has a very active imagination. My daughter even believes that the roots can curl up to act like snares and drink blood."

Dr. Brice smiled and continued to examine the tree.

"The roots are strange and I don't think they are a part of the tree. The rope like bark is unusual and is probably a vine that has embedded itself into the tree. I am guessing that the exposed roots also belong to the vine and not the tree. The twisted appearance of the trunk is probably from the parasitic vine. It seems to have spiraled around the tree like a piece of DNA and then kept up with the trees growth, but vines like this one nearly always kill the host tree. The strangling fig is an example but it bears fruit, which I don't see, and doesn't have thorns, which I do see. This tree is very much alive and appears to have benefited by being altered by the vine. It is difficult to tell whose roots are exposed, but my guess is that they belong only to the vine. It is also difficult to tell if the leaves belong to the vine or the tree, the branches are so knurled I can't tell whom they belong to, maybe both. My guess is the leaves belong to the tree. This is either a new species or the weirdest symbiotic arrangement I have ever seen."

"Is that the limb that impaled the father?"

I nodded in the affirmative and then pointed at the embedded chain saw.

"We are assuming that Floyd was trying to cut the tree down when the saw got stuck and that's when he got the sap on him. Can you identify the tree?"

"I wish I could," answered Dr. Brice, "but the trees shape and strange branching pattern doesn't fit into any genus that grows in these latitudes. It resembles a prehistoric plant. The leaves are a mix of evergreen and deciduous. It's a very strange arrangement. Do you know how long it has been here?"

I was almost embarrassed to answer. I knew only mythical accounts. Dr. Brice, however, was expecting a factual answer.

"According to Floyd's accounts of Indian lore, it has been here since the last Ice age."

I expected the scientist to laugh but it only spiked his interest.

"This is really fascinating." Dr. Brice replied. "I need to get pictures and samples. My kit is in the car. Do we have time for me to do a little investigating? I would like to collect samples of the sap, the leaves, the bark, and the roots."

"Take all the time you need." I replied. "Daphne can get your case from the car and I will help with the sampling. Just be careful, I've seen what this thing can do."

Daphne returned with Dr. Brice's case and a hatchet she found in the barn. "I thought you might need this," She said, and handed me the hatchet.

I reached out to take the hatchet but didn't get a good grip. It fell onto one of the exposed roots. Daphne reached down to pick it up but stopped short.

"Did you see that?" She shrieked. "It moved! I saw it move, the root twitched when the hatchet fell on it."

I started to question her but Dr. Brice stopped me.

"Repeat the experiment." He said emphatically. "Drop the hatchet on the root again."

I picked up the hatchet, and with all three of us concentrating on the root. I dropped it. This time several of the roots seemed to move. Dr Brice thought he saw a root twitch and Daphne swore she saw several roots react. I didn't agree. All I saw was dry dirt drop off a few roots when the hatchet hit, giving the appearance of movement. We tried the experiment again with similar results and couldn't reach an agreement.

Doctor Brice thought for a moment and gave us his opinion.

"Even though I thought I saw movement it is highly unlikely that the root moved, but there are carnivorous plants that do actually move and even seeds that walk and screw themselves into the ground. I'm not ruling it out and this may not be a plant at all. It may be a primitive animal, like a coral. This could be an important scientific find and until it can be studied in more detail we need to get it protected and I need to get a team in here."

I was in favor of further study, and for protecting the tree, but there were other considerations.

"This is a possible crime scene," I said, "and I'm not certain the police will allow a lot of scientists poking around, and we certainly don't need any more media hype."

"You have to understand how important this might be," replied Doctor Brice, "this may be an entirely new species. The implications are huge! I need to speak to the injured man to learn about the myths that go with this thing, and I need to get the University to back me on this."

"So much for putting a lid on it," Daphne observed. "Even I will have to report this sooner or later. I'm almost sorry I asked you to identify the tree. I thought the answer would be simple and would squelch all the hype but if you turn it into a scientific discovery, I don't know how long I can hold off."

"For Floyd's sake hold off as long as you can," I replied, "at least until Dr. Brice has real evidence and can describe this thing factually. A premature release will turn Floyd's farm into a circus. Do you both agree to keep things as quiet as possible for as long as possible?"

Both Daphne and Dr. Brice agreed.

CHAPTER TEN

It only took a few days for Doctor Brice's samples to be analyzed. The results attracted the immediate attention of the university's science department. The tree and its companion vine were indeed a new discovery, one with important implications.

Dr Brice informed me by phone that he and his associates determined that his initial assumption, that the tree was two distinct plants joined in a permanent relationship, was correct. The vine and the tree had grown together in a way that made them completely dependent upon each other.

"The vine and the tree," he explained, "benefit from their strange union by being able to ingest animal matter as well as by being able to absorb nutrients from the soil and use photosynthesis. The tree at the center of the union appears to be prehistoric and the vine almost as old."

"The University has claimed discovery rights and all rights for scientific access, so I may have lost control of how information is dispensed to the general public,"

This was bad news but everyone had to stand in line behind ongoing legal investigations. The scientists, the press, the need to preserve a potential crime scene, and the rights of private ownership, were all competing for access to the tree and by default, I had become the lawyer of record for the tree and its owner. I was now involved in much more than a simple criminal case.

The tree had definitely been responsible for the death of Floyd's father and was probably complicit in the death of Floyd's grandmother, but I couldn't prosecute a plant, and for me to serve my human client, I needed to expose the tree as having caused the death for which my human client was accused.

I was a tax lawyer, not a trial lawyer, and had never defended anyone in a criminal case. Legally the whole thing was ridiculous and it got worse by the day. I thought about calling an associate for help but didn't know any lawyers who had ever faced such a convoluted situation. I offered to find Floyd better council but he insisted that I continue.

Soon after Dr. Brice's team reported their initial findings, unsubstantiated news spread to the Ohio Center for Disease Control that a potentially dangerous plant was growing on a farm in Ohio. The first act of the Center for Disease Control was to request the entire farm quarantined until potential dangers from spores, wind borne seeds, creeping vines, and contaminated soil or other infected plants or animals could be ruled out.

If granted, the quarantine would play into the hands of the scientific community but would delay any further examinations of the crime scene and would probably contaminate any remaining evidence, cutting me off from findings I needed to build a defense for Floyd.

I filed a brief requesting a delay of quarantine until criminal investigations could be completed, stating the obvious fact that if the tree was as old as initial findings indicated, it had stood in the same spot for hundreds or thousands of years without contaminating the area. The OCDC granted me another two weeks of access to the tree with the stipulation that a protective wrap cover the tree immediately,

I expected a large sheet of saran wrap, but the bubble brought in to cover the strange plant was a discarded inflatable indoor golf driving range. The huge white inflatable dome was over 50 feet high and 200 feet in diameter. Inflated, it dominated the Brenner farm and dwarfed the tree. The dome was translucent, but artificial lights were added to mimic natural conditions. Like everything else surrounding the tree, the enclosure was overkill. It dominated the skyline and was visible from all the roads surrounding the Brenner farm. At night, the interior lights made the giant dome glow like a huge Christmas ornament.

Floyd's tree was now, in effect, under house arrest and quickly gained the attention of media everywhere. I had to take the whole thing seriously but, if I didn't have a client whose life was at stake, I would have found it laughable. As far as I was concerned it was all myth, but because of the intense attention focused on a small tree, standing on a small spot, on a small farm in Ohio, the myths were becoming the reality and I had to deal with them as if they were facts.

Investigations by various scientific teams were producing more theories than findings but, other than acidic sap, the scientists could find no reason to think the tree would contaminate its surroundings or suddenly propagate an invasive species. Most of the discoveries were mundane scientific stuff about an extremely rare and extremely old plant.

The first DNA results were also somewhat ordinary and indicated a linage tracing back to early plants in the Pleistocene, but there were also curious anomalies in its DNA. The genetic codes of the core tree and the invasive vine had overlapped and the vine and the tree shared chromosomes that would not have been common to both outside their symbiotic union. There were also gaps in the DNA sequence that standard tests couldn't explain.

CHAPTER ELEVEN

While Dr. Brice was outsourcing the genetic tests and dealing with research requests, I was preparing for Floyds arraignment hearing and Daphne was making frequent visits to the hospital.

Channel Three and The Gazette were both pressing Daphne for updated information. She continued to stall but couldn't hold out much longer. So far, the press knew only that Floyd was awaiting arraignment and that experts were examining the tree. Daphne and I were garnering additional facts but we both desperately needed Floyd's amnesia to turn into recollections. Unfortunately, Floyd's memories remained trapped behind a protective emotional barrier. I called Daphne twice a day hoping she was getting past his blocked memory.

"Daphne, have you made any progress? I'm running out of time."

Annoyed by my persistent calls, Daphne responded angrily.

"I'm doing the best I can." she answered. I visit Floyd twice a day and we are getting better acquainted. He trusts me and I actually enjoy our visits, but he still has a mental block."

"Can he be released from the hospital?" I asked.

"Not yet," Daphne responded. "His physical wounds are partially healed and, under normal circumstances, he could be released, but his psychological state and the suspicion that he was involved in his grandmother's death are keeping him in a restricted patient status. An ankle bracelet has replaced his handcuffs and he can move around and go to the cafeteria, but he can't leave the hospital."

I felt sorry for Floyd but I needed him healthy enough to attend his arraignment hearing. It had only been three weeks since his admittance to the hospital, but for a man as active as Floyd it must have seemed like an eternity. I had talked to Floyd's mother after the death of her husband and mother and, she too, had been damaged by the sudden extinction of her family. Floyd's mother had visited Floyd only once before committing herself to a clinic for grief counseling. Like Floyd, she needed to reestablish a sense of self. She needed a new attachment to society, new friends and a new purpose. Like Floyd, she needed the help of others and until she and her son could re-establish a solid psychological footing, they were of no help to each other.

Both had the help of professionals but Floyd had the additional help of a compassionate woman, a woman who seemed to be developing strong feelings for him.

Daphne continued to question Floyd hoping he would began to recall a few details but the memory of those few tragic moments remained buried and I suggested she avoid concentrating on the tragedies leading to Floyd's psychotic break and direct their conversations away from immediate realities.

Over the next few phone calls, Daphne told me that many of her conversations with Floyd centered on the importance of farming and that Floyd's basic philosophy was that farming was the creative activity from which all others developed.

"His ideas are somewhat childlike," Daphne reported, "They may be naïve, but his wisdom comes from an attention to detail missed by those with a better education. He sees the relationship between living things and the physical world as a bond created by a kind of universal force he calls, necessity".

"I have also learned," Daphne continued. "That Floyd's father was injured in a construction accident when Floyd was in the tenth grade. Floyd withdrew from school to help on the farm and his work routine quickly replaced his schooling. His education comes from real world experiences, not books, and his fresh perspective allows him see things hidden to others. His point of view is refreshing."

CHAPTER TWELVE

Floyd's arraignment hearing arrived before I was fully prepared. Requesting a delay could result in Floyd's transfer to a county jail and there was a chance that an early hearing might result in Floyd being released on his own recognizance. The prosecutor had only circumstantial evidence and other than a temporary loss of memory, Floyd's mental state was stable. The hearing was one day away and the results could be beneficial or disastrous, and Floyd had to be told that his grandmother was dead before it was disclosed in court.

Telling Floyd his grandmother was dead wasn't going to be easy and I was desperate to learn anything that would help me in court. With the hearing immanent, I called Daphne, hoping she might have new information.

We agreed to meet at the hospital and after a quick visit with Floyd, Daphne and I found the same table in the hospital cafeteria where we had dedicated ourselves to Floyd's defense three weeks earlier. As soon as we were seated, Daphne pulled the promissory spoon from her purse and placed it in the center of the table.

"Floyd is improving both physically and mentally," she began, "but I haven't been able to get anything that would help you with his case. I run errands for him so he doesn't go stir crazy, and I helped him get a special mask to cover the ugly scars on the side of his face. I also got him some gloves to cover the scary appearance of his hands and his grip is now either weak or very gentle when he holds my hand."

I paid close attention to Daphne's report and it gave me an idea.

"Can you get pictures of his scars? I can use them to create empathy for Floyd and present him as a victim rather than as a villain and, incidentally, why are you holding his hand? Is something developing between you and Floyd?"

Impulsively Daphne picked up the spoon and looked at the table to avoid my question.

I didn't want to admit it but I was jealous.

"That tells me a lot." I said. "Does he know you are developing feelings for him, and for that matter, are you aware of it?"

"I'm not sure," she answered.

Daphne folded her hands around the spoon.

"When is the hearing?" she asked.

"Tomorrow afternoon," I answered, "I'll need the photos in the morning and Floyd needs to be told about his grandmother before the hearing. I can't think of anyone better equipped to tell him than you."

"My God, No!"

Daphne dropped the spoon on the table.

"Think about it for a moment Daphne. You more than anyone know the details of what has happened and what is happening. Floyd doesn't even know why he is restricted to the hospital and he will have many questions. If you two have formed a bond, he must trust you. I know it isn't going to be easy but who else can do this?"

"How about asking the Doctor?" Daphne responded.

"It's up to you Daphne. Only you know how you feel about Floyd, and only you know if you are capable of doing this. Ask the Doctor to be in the room with you if you like, or have the Doctor tell him, but he has to be told today."

Daphne stood up. She had tears in her eyes and remained silent. She turned to go but I stopped her.

"Are you forgetting something?"

I pointed at the spoon.

Daphne didn't hesitate. She trembled as she picked up the spoon. It was obvious that she was falling in love with the Floyd.

"God I hate this spoon," she said.

Daphne knew what she had to do and that it would be almost impossible task. In a single afternoon, she had to get photographs of Floyd's injuries, tell him his grandmother was dead, and that he was being accused of killing her. There was a gap in Floyd's memory that she had to fill with terrible information and she wondered how Floyd would react. She had to be careful. She had to choreograph her presentation and steel her-self for the delivery of what could be a fatal blow to Floyd's sanity.

She went first to see Floyd's Doctor to explain the situation. The Doctor objected, fearing a complete withdrawal from reality but understood the necessity. Daphne also explained the need to get pictures of Floyd's blistered skin and asked the Doctor to arrange for photographs to be taken under the pretense of being needed for medical files. She also asked the Doctor if he could administer a tranquilizer before she told Floyd about his grandmother and requested that he be present when Floyd was told. The Doctor agreed and offered to give Daphne something to calm her nerves as well, but she refused, instead she went to the hospital chapel to prepare.

Daphne wasn't particularly religious but she had been brought up in a religious family. She would normally face difficult situations head on, but this one seemed beyond her ability. To gather her thoughts she sought the only quiet place in the hospital to prepare. She went to the chapel. She needed to say exactly the right things, she needed to maintain her composure and she hoped that God would help guide her words and steady her hand.

Daphne prayed in the chapel for almost an hour and then left for Floyd's room. At the door, she hesitated. She reached into her purse for the spoon to reinforce her commitment. When the hospital door opened, she put aside her doubts and took a deep breath.

The photos were ready and Floyd had been medicated. Floyd's Doctor directed her to a chair next to Floyd's bed and stepped back.

Floyd looked at Daphne and smiled.

"I'm glad you're here he said. I've been having some really weird dreams. Is my grandmother dead?"

Daphne was shocked. Had God answered her prayers? She took Floyd's hand, looked into his eyes and smiled.

"Yes Floyd, she is. She died of a heart attack trying to help you."

"I thought so." Floyd answered. "I had a dream, and in my dream she told me it wasn't my fault and that she is happy, and that I should try to be happy too. Do you believe in dreams?"

"I do now." Daphne answered. "Do you have any idea what your grandmother meant when she told you that it wasn't your fault."

"No, but I'm thinking it has something to do with my ankle bracelet."

"Your right", Daphne answered. No one has the whole story and, unfortunately, you can't remember. A lot of assumptions have been made and the police have concluded that you might have done something that caused your grandmother's death. They're holding you on suspicion, but your lawyer is trying to get the charges dropped and we're all trying to find out what really happened."

"Do you think I had anything to do with her death?" Floyd asked.

Floyd put his free hand on top of Daphne's hand. A flood of emotions made her blush. She tried desperately not to show her feelings and regain control. She stood up, bent over Floyd, and kissed him on his undamaged cheek.

"No I don't think you did anything wrong. You are a gentle man and wouldn't intentionally harm anyone."

"I agree." Said the Doctor,"

"Then what makes them think I had anything to do with it?" Floyd asked.

"We can get into the details later." Daphne replied. "And hopefully you can start to fill in the blank spots in your memory, but there were a couple earlier incidents that made them suspicious. Do you remember the fight with your neighbor?"

"Yes," Answered Floyd. "He made a remark about my Dad being a dumb farmer and had no business being on a snowmobile. I took a swing at him, but he dropped the assault charges."

Daphne answered carefully.

"It's just that you were involved in a violent act and the violence looks suspicious, especially with your memory loss."

"I think that's enough." The Doctor put his hand on Daphne's shoulder.

Daphne released Floyd's hand and told Floyd she would be back soon. The Doctor escorted Daphne to the door and handed her the photographs she had requested.

The meeting had drained Daphne emotionally and she took a moment to gather her thoughts before leaving the hospital. Her prayers had been to find the right words but Floyd had spoken them for her. Daphne didn't pray often but this seemed like a true miracle. Only Floyd's Grandmother could have supplied the truth to Floyd without creating an unbearable guilt, and she did it in a dream.

As a journalist, Daphne dealt with verifiable facts but Floyd's dream and Floyd's tree was taking her beyond her journalistic perspectives.

CHAPTER THIRTEEN

I met with Daphne to pick up the photographs and to get a report on how Floyd had taken the news. Daphne was hesitant to tell me about her prayers or Floyd's dream and limited her answers to what I needed to hear.

"Floyd knows his grandmother is dead." Daphne began. "He also knows that he is a suspect in her death. He took the news well and he understands why he is a suspect. He is certain that his grandmother's death was not his fault, but still hasn't recovered his memory. He's stable and can be released from the hospital as soon as the court allows."

I thanked her and headed for the courthouse. Because the case was so unusual, and because it was attracting so much attention, the Judge asked for initial arguments to be heard informally in his chambers. I welcomed the ruling. Without having to call witnesses, I had a chance to show the judge that the case against Floyd was based on assumptions and, hopefully, convince him to postpone or drop the charges pending additional evidence. The Prosecutor and I arrived at the Court House at the same time and entered the elevator together. The Prosecutor broke the silence as the elevator ascended.

"I may have enough circumstantial evidence to convince the judge that Floyd should be held pending formal charges unless you have something more solid that should be introduced."

The prosecutor cleared his throat and continued. "I'm willing to recommend that Floyd be released on his own recognizance if you will agree to keep an eye on him and, should he show symptoms of any mental instability, that you will notify me immediately. I will also need to be notified immediately of any recovery of memory."

I was unprepared for the prosecutor's offer but accepted his proposal without hesitation. Floyd would still be under suspicion but I would have additional time to fill in the gaps and try to clear up any remaining suspicions before an arraignment hearing was scheduled.

To insure the prosecutor wouldn't change his mind I showed him the photographs of Floyd's injuries as we stepped out of the elevator.

"My God" The Prosecutor commented. "It looks like someone took a blow torch to him. Are you certain this was caused by tree sap?"

"Very certain," I replied. The tree is being examined by a team from OSU and they have confirmed the caustic nature of the fluids from the tree."

"I have never heard of a poison tree," Replied the Prosecutor. "Do they know where it came from? I would hate to find one of these things growing in my back yard."

"Not yet." I replied. "There are poisonous trees in the tropics and some in England but none native to this area. Whatever it is, it's tough. The chain saw that's stuck in it cut nearly half way through but didn't kill it and the tree has already healed around the saw."

When we entered the Judge's chambers, the prosecutor spoke first.

"Your Honor, we have a dead seventy nine year old woman named Melisa Brenner whose cause of death is in question. A Deputy Sheriff found her lying on the ground outside her home with her grandson, twenty-eight year old Floyd Brenner, standing over her. I asked for an arraignment hearing because the circumstances surrounding her death are suspicious and I have reason to believe that manslaughter or a murder might have been committed. At the time, it seemed prudent to arraign Mr. Brenner on charges associated with his Grandmother's death but additional facts regarding this case have since come to light that may mitigate those charges. Until a more thorough investigation can take place, I am dropping my request for an immediate arraignment but Mr. Brenner is still a suspect and I request that his movement be limited until the investigation is complete. I also request that his lawyer, who is present, be made responsible for supervising the suspect's movements and for reporting any new information pertinent to this case immediately. The suspect is currently in the hospital and claims a complete memory loss regarding the events surrounding Mrs. Brenner's death. This alleged memory loss may be genuine or fabricated and in the interest of justice, I ask that an expert in the field be allowed to examine Mr. Brenner to determine if his loss of memory is real. With these stipulations in place, and with the agreement of Mr. Brenner's council, I recommend releasing the suspect on his own recognizance pending further actions."

After listening to the prosecutor's statement the Judge turned to me.

"Does Council for Mr. Brenner agree to the terms of the release?"

I agreed without any reservations.

The meeting in the Judge's chambers had taken only five minuets. Floyd was now free to leave the hospital but where would he go? Where could he go? I called Daphne with the good news and Daphne brought me up to date on Dr. Brice's progress regarding the tree.

"I hate to tell you this." Daphne began, "but when the police allowed the Botanist's team limited and supervised access to the tree to run tests, news leaks developed. Floyd's tree has become a celebrity and the Brenner Farm has once again become the focus of media attention."

"The scientific examinations have apparently given the legends Floyd told some credibility," Daphne continued, "and the deaths associated with the tree are making it front page news. The myths regarding the tree are rapidly replacing reality and the more people that read about the tree, the more the myths become real. The press has even solicited your daughter, and she has childishly embellished her stories without realizing that her stories would be reported as facts."

CHAPTER FOURTEEN

Floyd was about to be released from the hospital into a media frenzy. His farm and home were overrun with police, various fanatics, the press, and scientific investigators. Floyd's cattle had been moved to an adjacent farm where a neighbor was looking after them and it was doubtful they would ever be able to return to their home pastures. The once peaceful Brenner farm was now the focus of worldwide attention.

Because of Floyd's tree, the farm had become a new frontier for scientists, and because of the myths, the farm had become a tabloid holy site for the media. Floyd couldn't live on the farm while the hysteria persisted, and the media myths were gaining such notoriety that Floyd might never be able to return to his beloved farm.

Floyd's first wish, after his release from the hospital, was to go home and he asked Daphne to take him to the farm. Floyd was unaware of the turmoil the events surrounding his grandmother's death, and the tree had created. He only knew he was free and could go where he wanted as long as he remained in the local area. He knew his life was changed. He knew his father and grandmother were dead and that his mother was gone, but he still wanted to return to the security and fond memories cloistered in the old farmhouse. But things had changed so drastically that a return was impossible.

Daphne knew what Floyd would face when he walked out of the hospital. She wanted to protect him, but knew she couldn't. The press would be waiting, shouting inconsiderate questions that would hurt him, and they would be relentless. They would be ruthless, believing the public's right to know trumped personal rights. Daphne was an experienced part of the media wolf pack and had done her share of ripping at individuals to get a story, but she was now on the other side. She knew what to expect but wasn't sure how to shield the sensitive naïve man she had taken under her wing. She had made promises she might not be able to keep and she would feel his pain when he saw his farm being trampled. She would also feel his desperation when he realized he could never go home and would share his fear when the media wolves attacked. She couldn't protect him, but maybe she could prepare him.

Daphne approached Floyd and put her hand on his arm. "Before you leave the hospital we need to talk."

"What do we need to talk about?" Floyd replied. "I just want to get out of here and go home."

"That is exactly what we need to talk about. I may not be able to take you home and you may not want to go there, at least not yet."

"Why not"? Floyd asked.

Floyd stopped pushing his clothes into the plastic bag the hospital had given him and straightened up. He was much taller than Daphne and she had to tip her head back to talk to him. She sat down on the side of the hospital bed, took Floyd's hand and motioned for him to sit beside her.

"The stories about the tree and about your grandmother's death have attracted the news media and there are a lot of reporters roaming around. The

109

police still have your house and barn taped off to keep people away and there are experts examining the tree. You probably won't be able to return to your farm until the police finish investigating, and with all the people around, you probably don't want to go there."

"What about my cattle," Floyd pleaded. "What about Chopin?"

"They are being taken care of and your farm equipment is being guarded. Your things are safe. People who don't belong are being kept off your property but they wander around the parameter. You can visit but you can't go home. Do you understand?"

Floyd understood but he didn't agree.

"It's my farm and I should be able to go home. What about my lawyer, what does he say?"

Daphne immediately called me and explained the situation. Unfortunately, I had no immediate solution. The farm was technically Floyd's property and he had the right to occupy it and refuse entry to others, but he couldn't refuse entry to the police, especially since it had been declared a crime scene. So far, the prosecutor hadn't pressed charges and the police had been allowed two more weeks of free access to the farm, long enough for an investigation. I had a good argument for forcing the removal of the crime scene tape, and without a new court ruling Floyd could order everyone else to leave, but did I want to do that? I doubted if Floyd was stable enough to live alone and doubted that he could stay stable in close proximity to the tree. I had been mandated by the court to maintain a close watch on Floyd and I wouldn't be able to watch him if he lived several miles out of town.

I needed to convince him to live closer, at least temporarily, but where?

While I waited for Floyd and Daphne, I called a realtor friend to elicit her help in finding a place in town. I also called the judge to clarify Floyd's right to access his property and occupy the farm. The judge could find no reasons for Floyd to be restricted from his property unless formal charges were brought, but cautioned me about loosing control or unintentionally creating an untenable situation for Floyd or myself. With all the media attention, creating an untenable situation was a definite possibility.

Daphne had been a great help in dampening inflammatory news releases, but she was under pressured from her employers to stop chaperoning the object of the story and start covering the story itself.

Daphne couldn't keep her commitment to the dirty spoon forever and I had to face the fact that in addition to being Floyd's lawyer I had become Floyd's guidance councilor.

Floyd was scheduled to be released from the hospital just before noon. I suggested lunch as a way to reintroduce Floyd to his freedom, and to discuss Floyd's immediate future. I selected a small restaurant on the quiet side of town and waited for them to arrive.

Daphne and Floyd managed to get out of the hospital and through the hospital-parking garage without being recognized, but on their way to the restaurant, out of town reporters spotted and followed them. They walked into the restaurant directly behind Daphne and Floyd.

One of the reporters approached Floyd before they could be seated. I tried to intervene but was too late. Before I could react, the reporter pushed a hand held recorder in Floyd's face and began asking questions. The reporter's friend started taking pictures.

The intrusion startled Floyd and he pushed the recorder away.

"What the hell are you doing?" he shouted.

His shout attracted the attention of others in the restaurant, many of them friends of Floyd.

The reporter shoved the recorder back in Floyd's face and in a very offensive manner asked, "How does it feel to be released from custody? Have you been back to the farm?"

Floyd reacted and swatted the recorder away with the back of his gloved hand. The recorder flew across the room and Floyd folded his hand against his chest in pain. The reporter objected loudly and tried to continue his unwanted interrogation but he had overlooked the fact that he wasn't in a big city.

In a small town people know each other and look out for each other. Before the reporter and his photographer could move, half a dozen restaurant patrons were on there feet and literally tossed the two intruders out onto the street. The reporters stood outside screaming something about suing for assault, which brought laughter from the restaurant crowd.

If the reporters wanted to bring charges for being tossed out, they would have to gather names by coming back inside, or call the local police, who would side with the patrons. The reporters chose the wiser course and left.

One of the individuals that helped the unwelcome reporters find the exit came over to Floyd and apologized for the trouble. Floyd recognized him as one of his tradesman friends and reached out to shake his hand, but realized it was gloved, and withdrew it.

"Thanks George," he said, "I could have handled it but my hands are still sore."

"Don't worry about it," George replied, "We've got your back."

After we seated ourselves in a corner booth, Floyd looked across the table at me.

"Is that going to happen often?" he asked.

"Probably," I replied, "and if you push or even touch one of them you will probably end up in jail."

Floyd looked puzzled. "Do you mean to tell me that just because someone is a reporter they can push things in your face, and question you anytime they want? That's like giving bullies a free pass to kick kids around on the playground. Somebody's sure to get hurt."

Daphne took over the conversation.

"It's not right, but it's going to happen, and it will happen a lot. You need to ignore the reporters. You're at the center of a story that everyone is interested in. They want to know everything about you and about the tree. They want to know what happened to your grandmother. You want to know the same things, and even though we all want to know what happened, you can't afford to loose your temper. It will make you look like a violent man. We know you're not violent but the police aren't sure. Do you understand how important it is to control yourself and ignore them?"

Floyd stared at the menu and I thought it wise to change the conversation but before I could begin, my realtor friend called on my cell phone. She had found an upstairs furnished apartment in an old but well kept Victorian home not far from the restaurant.

"That was a friend of mine," I said, "she has found a place in town for us to look at that might be a good place for you to stay until you can go home. It's not far from here and I think we should look at it."

Floyd objected but Daphne made him understand and promised to check on him often.

CHAPTER FIFTEEN

We went directly from the restaurant to the address given me by the realtor. A well-known local artist and retired art teacher, named Julia, owned the home.

Julia knew about the tree and about Floyd being a suspect in his grandmother's death but agreed to show us the apartment and make up her own mind about Floyd.

When we pulled up in front of the grand old Victorian house Floyd commented on how much it resembled his grandmother's house, except for the obvious fact it was in much better shape. The grounds around the house were meticulously kept and beautifully landscaped with well-manicured bushes and many flowers. There was a large covered front porch with an octagonal room off to one side with an eight sided tower room above.

Julia met us at the door and welcomed us inside. I introduced Daphne and Floyd and Julia took us to the octagonal parlor. She directed us to seats and offered us tea. Her formality was enchanting and while she prepared the tea, we explored adjacent rooms. The furniture matched the Victorian architecture and although antique, looked new. The living room had ornate oak trim and an oak plank floor with a beautiful oriental rug in the center. Off to one side there was a grand piano and in the next room were hundreds of books neatly arranged on decorative wooden shelves. Floyd was intrigued. This was a style of living he had never experienced. Books, music, order and beauty filled the house and fit perfectly into its architecture.

When Julia came back with the tea, Floyd asked if he could touch the piano.

"Do you play?" Julia asked

"A little," Floyd replied, "I taught myself"

"Do you need music?" Julia asked, "I don't have much popular music. My dear departed husband was a classical musician and most of what I have is classical."

Floyd seated himself at the piano and asked if she had a particular etude by Chopin.

"I may," Julia answered, "but it will take me a while to find it."

"It's Ok," Floyd replied, as he adjusted the piano seat, "I think I can remember it."

Daphne was in disbelief and turned to me with an astonished look on her face. She obviously didn't know about Floyd's musical abilities.

"This is good I whispered. If his memory is this good he may remember other things."

Floyd played the etude, and in spite of his gloved hands, made only a few mistakes. He played with grace and feeling and it brought tears to Julia's eyes.

"Oh my," Julia sobbed, "There hasn't been any music like that in this house since my husband died. Oh Floyd I do hope you will come and live here."

Daphne was less formal in expressing her astonishment.

"You have to be shitting me." She blurted out. "Where did he learn to play like that, and how did he memorize such a difficult piece?"

When we had all recovered from Floyd's performance, Julia gave us a tour of the rest of the house. Julia's bedroom was on the first floor, along with a kitchen and an artist's studio with lots of glass for light. In the studio were her brushes, her paints, and several easels. Her own paintings hung on the walls in the parlor. Paintings by her former students hung on both sides of the hallway leading to the studio. They were mostly landscapes or still life but included a few portraits. The paintings made Julia's fame as a painter and as a teacher evident. They were masterpieces and Floyd hesitated in front of each of them, soaking in their beauty.

It took very little convincing to get Floyd to agree to move into Julia's upstairs apartment. The suite was sometimes used as a bed and breakfast and was fully furnished, including dishes and cooking utensils. Floyd would have an outside entrance by way of a private set of stairs, his own kitchen and bath, a bedroom and the tower room. He loved the tower room and promised Julia that he would help take care of the grounds and help her keep the house in repair. I drew up a simple rental agreement, helped them decide on a reasonable month to month fee and after only one night in a nearby motel, Floyd was ready to gather a few belongings from his Grandmother's house and move to what he described as a refuge in history, a place from a golden age before the world became twisted.

I drove Floyd to the farm but was concerned he might react badly to the dome and to all the strangers. Daphne came along just in case.

CHAPTER SIXTEEN

When Floyd, Daphne and I arrived at the Brenner farm, we found a sheriff's car and several Federal vans parked near the barn.

I assumed the Sheriff and the Federal officials were at the tree and wanted to get Floyd's things and get away before anything could trigger a relapse. I also wanted to see if being home might prompt Floyd to recall any forgotten events but, for the moment, getting Floyd relocated to a stable environment took precedence and I tried to hurry things along.

Floyd motioned toward the empty vehicles.

"What are these people doing here?"

I answered quickly, trying to deflect his attention.

"The scientists are examining the tree to determine its species, and the Sheriff is here to protect your property. We should get your things and let them do their job. I can bring you back another day to take a closer look at the farm."

Floyd wasn't buying it. He wouldn't be rushed and started walking in the direction of the tree. Daphne put her hands up in despair and started after him. I made one more verbal appeal, gave up, and followed them.

Floyd was walking fast and out distanced Daphne and me easily. He reached the soybean patch and when he saw the giant dome covering the tree, he stopped and stood transfixed.

"What the hell is That?" He exclaimed.

The dome looked like a giant quilted igloo. The futuristic structure was so large and so out of place in a rural agricultural setting that it was frightening. Floyd stood frozen. When Daphne and I caught up, we stood next to him. We all stood transfixed by the strange monument that had been erected over the tree. The huge inflatable structure gave the tree an importance well beyond the simple stories told by Floyd and well beyond its peculiar biology.

Floyd spoke first.

"Are they trying to hide it? Are they afraid it will escape? What are they doing? My father's blood is in the ground under the tree and this is my property. I don't want that thing on my property!"

As Floyd spoke, the Sheriff emerged from a tube like entrance on the side of the dome. He was surprised when he saw us and immediately motioned for us to follow him. He led us a short distance back along the path we had just traversed and pointed at a small patch of weeds and told us what to look for.

"One of the scientists working on the tree came out for a smoke and discovered something just a few minutes ago. I've called for our forensic team to photograph and catalog it and they are on their way."

"As Floyd's lawyer you need to see what we found and maybe Floyd can tell us why it's out here."

The Sheriff urged us closer to the edge of the weed patch. He let us approach close enough to look into the weeds but held his arm out to keep us from stepping on the evidence. At the edge of the weeds, in a small depression, was a cane.

"It's Grandma's cane." Floyd shouted, and then in a quiet voice.

"Oh my God, I remember."

"I tried to help her." Floyd exclaimed and reached for the cane. The Sheriff stopped him.

"I saw her lying here," Floyd continued, "I picked her up and carried her back to the house. I tried to save her."

The Sheriff seized on the opportunity to interrogate Floyd and asked me if he could ask my client a few questions.

I asked Floyd. "Are you up to answering questions?"

"Will it get me in more trouble?"

"Not if you did nothing wrong."

The Sheriff chimed in.

"Floyd, you said it was your fault. What did you mean?

"I meant that if I hadn't acted crazy, she wouldn't have chased me out here when I tried to cut down the tree. If I would have calmed down she wouldn't have had a heart attack."

"How do you know it was a heart attack?" asked the Sheriff.

"Daphne told me." Floyd answered.

The Sheriff continued his interrogation.

"What did you do while you were acting crazy?"

"I remember I was feeling really depressed." Floyd answered. "It was the first day of hunting season and I wanted to go hunting with my dad, but he was dead. I got my rifle and thought that if I pretended dad was with me it might make me feel better."

"Did it?" I asked

"No" Floyd answered. "It made me feel worse. I hiked out past the cornfield and spotted a doe with a couple fawn near the tree. The tree made me mad and I almost shot the doe."

"Why didn't you?" The Sheriff asked.

"I realized what I was doing and it made me sick," Floyd continued."

"If I killed the doe I would be a monster like the tree and I almost pulled the trigger. I cursed at the tree and it spooked the deer. The doe ran under the tree, caught her hoof in one of the tree's roots and went down. I could tell her leg was broken and knew I had sentenced her fawns to death. I tried to shoot them to save them from the coyote. I got one but missed the other."

"I felt really bad, and I carried the dead fawn back to the barn, why I'm not sure. I thought I got my knife to gut and skin it, but I had gotten my chain saw instead. I must have been in a daze because I mutilated the fawn. I remember Grandma screaming at me and chasing me out toward the tree. I wanted to kill the tree with the chain saw but it was too tough. The saw got stuck and I had to give up. The tree sap that splattered from the saw was burning my face and hands but I heard grandma behind me. I saw her collapse right here."

Floyd pointed at the cane

"I tried to wake her up but I couldn't. I carried her over my shoulder back near the house. I remember calling 911 and riding in an ambulance.

"Do you remember the police cars and my deputy trying to get you to calm down?"

"No, the next thing I remember was waking up in the hospital."

After Floyd finished, it all made sense. Floyd had made two trips to the tree. On the first he had taken and left his rifle and took the fawn back to the barn to gut. On the second trip Grandma tried to stop him but the effort was too much for her heart. She collapsed in the weeds where they found her cane. The bruises on grandma's chest and her broken ribs were from being carried over Floyd's shoulder, not from a beating.

Floyd was innocent. He had suffered a mental breakdown and had acted irrationally but he wasn't guilty of any crime and the Sheriff seemed to agree.

I urged Floyd to get his things so I could get back and speak to the prosecutor. After a short delay, while Floyd checked the barn and gathered some clothing, we were on our way back to town.

CHAPTER SEVENTEEN

Daphne helped Floyd take his belongings to his new apartment, the Sheriff reported the discovery of the cane and of Floyd's recovered memory and I arranged a meeting with the prosecutor.

I expected the prosecutor to drop all charges, but to my chagrin, he thought it wise to reduce the charges but not dismiss them. I argued, but it was futile. The prosecutor was adamant. If Floyd had not acted irrationally, his grandmother would still be alive. He was therefore still complicit in causing her death. The prosecutor was unsure of what charges he would bring but insisted on convening a grand jury to decide on an indictment. Floyd could remain free under my supervision but with restrictions.

I hurried to Floyd's new apartment expecting to find him in an emotional state. Instead, I found him playing the piano while Daphne listened and drank tea. He stopped playing when I entered the room.

"Thank you for taking care of me." He said. "I would never have remembered what happened without your help. I miss my Grandma, I even missed her funeral, but she forgave me in a dream, and now I remember trying to save her. Thank you."

I assured Floyd that I would continue to look out for him and his farm, and asked him to learn a new piece of music so my daughter and I could come to another recital. He enthusiastically agreed and resumed playing. Daphne walked me to the door.

She spoke in a soft voice so Floyd couldn't hear.

"I have to start reporting on the story or I will lose my job. I hope this won't interfere with your case, but I have no choice. I plan to see Floyd often as a friend and I promise not to take advantage of my relationship with him. I can run all of my stories by you before I send them in. Are you ok with that?"

I was confident Daphne would keep me informed without my needing to track every development and the next day I received an advanced copy of her upcoming press release.

To help tone down the hysteria, Daphne had tried her best to keep most of the details regarding Floyd's arraignment out of the public eye, but she couldn't hold back any longer. Other reporters were uncovering details and the tree continued to be big news.

Without facts, the tabloids were dependent on rumors and were publishing wild stories. Floyd was portrayed either as a psychopath that worshiped a tree possessed by evil spirits, or as a deranged farmer suspected of killing his grandmother. The tree was either depicted as an evil spirit with roots, or as a poisonous mutant created by mad scientists. My daughter's imaginative accounts of the tree added to the problem. The press continued to invent fantasy accounts and the public continued to believe them.

Floyd managed to escape the hysteria by retreating into the quiet world of music, art and literature inside his new home. The police kept the press and radical protestors away and it became a perfect sanctuary. Inside, Floyd was safe. Outside, the clamor continued.

Whenever the excitement subsided, another incident grabbed the media's attention.

The latest occurred when a tabloid photographer bribed a farmer across the road from the Brenner farm to let him climb to the top of the farmer's silo and use a telescopic lens to photograph the scientists as they took equipment and samples in and out of the dome.

Unfortunately, the photographer's attempt to obtain exclusive photos ended in disaster. The photographer used no safety equipment to scale the silo and when he reached the top, he slipped and fell to his death.

The photographer's camera captured two photographs of the dome before he fell and one dramatic picture of the screaming photographer on his way down. The pictures provided a sensationalized epitaph for the over zealous reporter, and when they appeared on the front pages of major newspapers, they rekindled the media frenzy.

"Devil Tree in Ohio claims third victim as reporter falls to death trying to photograph secret tests."

In Columbus, Ohio, the Governor became concerned that bad press and the intervention of the Federal Government might have a negative impact on the image of Ohio. Anything happening in his State important enough to get the attention of the Feds was something he needed to address.

The Governor summoned Dr Brice and a geneticist helping Dr. Brice to the State House. When the two scientists arrived, they were ushered into the Governor's office. The doors were closed and a guard was posted to keep the press away.

"Is all this silliness really necessary?" The Governor began. "A new plant species may be remarkable but hardly warrants this much attention, and why did the CDC impose quarantine? I understand the public being interested in the unexplained death of a grandmother but the press has created a monster out of that damn tree, and you people are making it worse. Why are you so interested?"

"It's not just a new species." Dr. Brice answered, "It's a very strange and very rare plant. The tree we have under the dome has unusual genetic patterns. What they are for, and what they do, we are trying to discover. We think only one of the symbiotic pair of plants is responsible for the unusual chromosomes, but the plants share genetic material so we can't be certain."

It was obvious to the geneticist that the Governor's eyes were beginning to glaze over but Dr. Brice ignored the Governor's inattention and continued.

"We know the sap from the symbiotic vine is very acidic and that the pair has been alive for an extremely long time. The two plants share genes and are physically joined, which may have something to do with their longevity. We have only begun to investigate, but the tree has genetic patterns that haven't been found anywhere else in nature."

The Governor rocked back in his chair and laughed.

"I've heard some wild stories but this one takes the cake. You guys better take out your hankies and wipe off your microscope lenses before you start kicking up dust by claiming an alien has landed. Just because you've found unusual genes in an old plant doesn't mean anything."

Dr. Brice and the geneticist had expected the Governor to react to the news of an important scientific find with at least some interest. Instead, he instantly threw up a barrier to keep out any new ideas and expressed no curiosity at all.

"You scientists get real excited when you find something you can't figure out and make a big deal out of it. I've been following the news, and you have yourselves panting like dogs, running around a tree that isn't going anywhere. A couple tragic accidents happened on that farm and the press and the police jumped on them. Now you're making things worse by trying to turn the tree into a science project."

"For God's sake," the Governor continued, "the tree just stood there and got run into, and a grieving son went a little berserk. I don't care how old it is it's still just a tree, and if God wants to add a couple strange genes it's his prerogative. The kind of press you are stirring up makes Ohio look bad. One newspaper even said the tree drank blood like a vampire."

The Governor stood up, put both hands on his desk and leaned forward.

"I'm directing the Ohio CDC to remove the bubble and get rid of the tree before Ohio gets any more bad press, and I would appreciate it if you and the other science guys would clam up and go home."

Dr. Brice and the geneticist were stunned. Without shaking hands, the Governor turned and left the room.

The scientists had been chastised like children and summarily dismissed.

"What the hell was that?" The geneticist asked.

"That was a good old boy Governor doing his best to keep Ohio in the 19th Century." Replied Dr. Brice, "I don't think we're going to get much support from him and unless you have a lot of leverage in Washington, we may be packing up real soon."

"Do you think we could be exaggerating the importance of our findings?" The geneticist asked.

"Hell no," Brice answered, "We've found the oldest living thing ever discovered and it has genetic variants that are very strange. Either we have proof of a new form of life, or the most extreme mutation ever found. The press wants to exaggerate the evidence, the Governor wants to bury it, and the fanatics want to worship it. All we want to do is understand it, but if the Governor has his way we'll never get the chance."

"Your right," The geneticist answered. "And it isn't the evidence that frightens him, it's the implications. The discovery has the potential to kick the props out from under many entrenched scientific beliefs, but before we create a real mess, we need to be certain that were on solid ground. We need to be certain that we aren't just creating our own myth."

Both scientists agreed on the need for caution. They didn't agree on the interpretation of their findings.

Dr. Brice interpreted the strange pairing of the tree and vine, the overlapping genetics, and the unusual genetic arrangements, as an extreme and very rare mutation with the ability to live without aging, but an inability to reproduce.

The geneticist had a more extreme vision, one closer to the imaginary stories told by a ten year old. He entertained the idea that the seed, for at least one of the genetically joined pair, could be extraterrestrial. The vine contained the most amino acid pairs and was the geneticist's candidate for an extraterrestrial origin. Dr Brice argued against the alien life theory believing an early evolutionary life form had evolved in parallel with a more common life form, had become extinct, and left only one final example.

It was doubtful that any evidence gathered to date would prove either theory correct. The only certainty was that the unusual characteristics of the tree were scientifically significant, and would reshape many important scientific principles.

After the visit with the Governor, a quick stop at the tree, and a short interview with Daphne, Dr. Brice flew back to OSU, and the geneticist flew back to Washington.

The scientific truth about the tree was being sought inside a white plastic inflatable dome by a team of scientific investigators. Outside the dome there were only wild stories, each more bizarre than the next. The tree was an evil spirit, a sign from god, an extreme mutant, even a secret weapon. The worst offenders in the race to create news had moderated their efforts as the stories became repetitive, but the tree was still attracting fanatics. Daphne used her short interview with the scientists to reshape her next broadcast, and true to her word; I received an advanced copy of her upcoming news release.

In contrast to other exaggerated reporting, Daphne's report was based on mundane facts. Her first hand information was so tame that I chuckled as I read it.

Channel Three News report for 7PM Wednesday by Daphne Collins:

"It has been more than a month since a set of strange circumstances turned an ordinary farm in Ohio into the focus of an intense scientific investigation and an ongoing legal battle. The huge protective bubble you see behind me covers a mysterious tree that is at the center of all this excitement and it is becoming more interesting by the day. Scientists examining the tree have found it to be older than any tree discovered before and that it has a genetic arrangement different from other plants. All this excitement began with a nine- one- one call from Floyd Brenner asking for help, saying the tree had killed his grandmother. Myths about this strange plant go back to prehistoric times and modern day soothsayers are adding more myths every day. Legal battles are developing over the ownership of the tree and scientists from the Federal Government have become involved.

Floyd Brenner, who owns the farm, remains in seclusion. He is accused of being partly responsible for his grandmother's death, an accusation he denies. A variety of demonstrators continue to bring their diverse causes to the scene in the hope of getting their message on TV and the curious who circle the farm are creating traffic problems. My advice to viewers is to stay tuned as I continue to bring you the latest developments. The only thing you can see from the highway is the protective bubble and homemade signs held by demonstrators, most of which have little to do with the tree or actual events."

***

My initial humorous reaction to Daphne's mundane broadcast soon proved misplaced. The discoveries made regarding the unusual genetic patterns were about to overshadow even the most extreme claims made by the tabloid press.

CHAPTER EIGHTEEN

Daphne finished her broadcast, returned to her apartment, entered her notes into her laptop, and checked her next day's schedule. She wanted to see Floyd and hoped she wasn't becoming a pest. In addition to Floyd's renewed interest in music, he had started taking art lessons from his famous landlady.

Daphne was curious about his new interest in art and her feelings for Floyd were growing stronger as his new personality emerged. The anger Floyd had displayed after his father's death had begun to mellow as he read from the classics on his landlady's bookshelves. As Floyd's intellectual and artistic talents developed, a sophisticated charm began to compliment the folk wisdom that made Floyd endearing,

To cover his scars and disfigured left cheek, Floyd continued to ware the gloves and mask Daphne had given him. Daphne wasn't in the least repelled by Floyd's damaged skin but found the mask and gloves to be attractive cosmetic additions. She was falling in love with Floyd but didn't want to reveal her emotions until she knew Floyd had reciprocal feelings. Daphne was attractive and other men often showed an interest, but Daphne was too busy to be distracted by an active dating life, and remained focused on her job.

Daphne arrived at Julia's house to see Floyd late in the afternoon.

"I've never seen anyone with this much raw talent," Julia said as she let Daphne in through the front door.

"I showed him how to hold the pallet, how to mix a few basic colors and how to prepare a canvas and he immediately sketched out a composition and began to paint. I coach him on brush techniques and answer his questions on establishing depth and background, but he paints as if he has painted with oils before."

Julia led Daphne to the studio and pointed at the canvas Floyd was working on. Floyd stepped back to let the women see his painting.

"Look at what he has created in just a few hours. It's quite remarkable."

Daphne recognized the tree immediately, but instead of the sinister appearance she remembered from her own visits to the farm, the tree on the canvas had a placid, almost serene appearance. The dead deer she remembered under the tree was absent and the early morning light Floyd had painted as a background gave the tree a look of rugged persistence rather than foreboding. A broken tree limb was reaching out as if it were trying to tell the observer something, and the twisted vine she remembered as sinister, was wrapped around the tree's trunk in a soft embrace. The tree on the canvas wasn't at all like the tree that had killed Floyd's father and driven Floyd mad, and yet it was the same tree. It was the same tree forgiven. It was the same tree understood, no longer feared or hated. Floyd's remarkable talents included more than just the ability to create masterpieces out of brick and mortar or to play the piano or to paint, it included the ability to forgive and in his first remarkable painting, Floyd had forgiven himself and the tree.

Floyd watched the expression on the two women's faces as they scrutinized the result of his first attempt to bring a canvas to life. Julia was in awe and Daphne was in tears. Floyd hugged them both.

CHAPTER NINETEEN

In spite of Floyd's recovered memory, enough doubt remained for the prosecutor to ask for a grand jury to decide if the case should move forward. Floyd was being accused of second-degree manslaughter, a lesser charge because the case was based entirely on circumstantial evidence. A date was set for an open grand jury to convene, and before I felt fully prepared, we were in court and the gavel sounded.

I had the same evidence as the prosecutor but interpreted it in a way that made Floyd a victim of a psychotic break, a break that made him unaware that his grandmother was in jeopardy. Instead of having caused his grandmother's death, he had tried to save her.

The prosecutor saw the evidence differently and expressed his view in his opening statement.

"Ladies and gentlemen of the jury," the prosecutor began, "you have been selected to decide a point of law, to decide if the evidence presented warrants an indictment. You are not here to decide which lawyer is better or how much sympathy the defendant is due. An elderly woman is dead because of the actions of others. She did not die peacefully in bed or in a hospital. She died in an open field not far from her house. The defendant's lawyer will try to explain her death as an accident resulting from a chain of events that could not have been anticipated or controlled. Some of those events are indisputable but some are open to interpretation and need to be questioned. The relevant facts of Melisa Brenner's death however are clear. The events that took place immediately prior to her death were preventable and except for the indifference of the defendant, Melisa Brenner would be alive today. The law is clear and the facts are clear. Don't be confused by sympathetic arguments. Your job is to decide a simple point of law based upon facts."

Floyd sat next to me dressed in a suit and tie. His beard was neatly trimmed and his mask and gloves were in place. The mask covered the left side of his face and the jury was to his right and could see his facial expressions.

I was aware of Floyd's tendency to react emotionally and counseled him repeatedly to remain placid. Any strong show of emotion could work against him. The prosecutor had just stressed the importance for the jury to remain dispassionate and to arrive at their decision using only the facts, but I knew, in spite of his admonitions, that he would attempt to evoke emotional responses and use them to his advantage.

The courtroom was as much theatre as it was logic and the prosecutor was a better dramatist than I was, and in this respect, he had the advantage. I had offered to find Floyd better council several times but he refused.

After his opening remarks, the prosecutor took his seat and I approached the jury. I had studied the jury members briefly but now, standing just a few feet away looking into their faces, I could make eye contact and read their attitudes. Some showed anticipation, waiting to see what I would say, others looked away trying to avoid the responsibility for another human being's fate, and others looked defiant as if this were a game where it was important for them to be on the winning side.

Nearly all of my experience as a lawyer was with the simple preparation of tax documents, negotiating settlements and an occasional divorce where a judge would decide the outcome based upon a learned opinion. The importance of the jury system as a cornerstone in our democratic system was ingrained into my psyche during law school, but now, facing the vagaries reflected in the faces in front of me, the jury took on the uncertainty of a casino. I felt like I was gambling, more than arguing for the truth and I began my opening remarks hesitantly.

"The prosecutor is correct. You will be asked to render a decision. You will be asked to decide if there is sufficient evidence to charge Mr. Brenner with manslaughter. You have been instructed by the judge to follow the law in reaching your decision but facts are sometimes slippery, the law is sometimes vague, and you are not just deciding which side wins you are deciding if an individual should face trial for a serious crime. If the facts were always clear and the law simple all of this would be unnecessary. We don't act out our lives in a vacuum. Circumstances are constantly affecting us and directing us. None of you volunteered to be here. Circumstances brought you here in the same way that circumstances brought Floyd Brenner here. If we are going to ignore the circumstances surrounding this case we might as well take a vote now or toss a coin and go home. Floyd loved his grandmother and is still grieving for her. He is the victim of circumstances that have left a permanent mark on his heart and on his face and hands. Melisa Brenner is dead but Floyd didn't cause her death any more than your best friend caused you to be here. Listen carefully, judge fairly, and remember, this isn't a game, your individual decisions don't add up to a score, they will determine the fate of another human being."

As I sat down Floyd twisted in his seat so he could see me past his mask. He didn't speak but there was a question in the expression on his face. My remarks to the jury were intended to rebut the prosecutor's implication that a decision to indict would be a simple decision based on a few facts. My rebuttal also made it clear to Floyd, that the optimism he had brought into the courtroom might be misplaced. My remarks made him realize that the outcome of his trial wasn't certain and there was a real possibility that he could be indicted regardless of what he knew to be true.

The prosecutor would follow a logical pattern of selective evidence presentation and directed witness testimony leaving out facts or opinions that were contrary to his case. In an adversarial justice system, it would be up to me to fill in the missing pieces so the jury could make a rational decision. Both the prosecutor and I knew that theater would play as large a part as logic in leading the jury to a decision. Truth would be only one of many factors in determining the outcome.

Because of the judge's unusual decision allowing observers, the courtroom was filled with a diverse crowd of friends, fanatics and the curious. Reporters and photographers pressed up against each other along the back and sidewalls with instructions to be quiet but their very presence was distracting. I tried to get the judge to keep the proceedings closed but my request was denied. Any overreaction, every word and every ruling, would now instantly be broadcast outside the courtroom.

Floyd was an unwilling celebrity facing an unwarranted charge and possible prison time. With Floyd, in his mask and gloves, the proceedings were taking on aspects of a sideshow with an interesting freak on display. I had to play to the press as well as the jury if I were to have a chance of proving that an indictment wasn't warranted.

As his first witness, the prosecution called the Deputy Sheriff who had been first on the scene. As soon as the Deputy was sworn by the court to tell the truth, the direction the prosecutor would take became clear.

"Deputy, when you arrived at the Brenner farm on the day of Melisa Brenner's death, what did you observe?"

"I saw a large man standing over a woman on the ground. He was screaming something unintelligible and pulling at his beard."

"Is the man you saw in the court room?" The Deputy answered in the affirmative and pointed at Floyd.

"Did you make an immediate attempt to restrain the man?"

"No, he seemed completely out of control and I knew backup would be there in a few seconds so I waited"

"Did the man notice you? Did he know you were there?"

"I don't know"

"When you drove up did you have your siren on?"

"Yes"

"Could anyone with normal hearing as close to your car as the defendant, not have heard the sound of your siren?"

I could see where the prosecutor was going and objected to his question.

"Your honor we all agree that police sirens are loud but the Deputy cannot possibly testify as to the state of mind or the state of Mr. Brenner's hearing at that moment. It calls for speculation."

The Judge hesitated for a moment, then ruled in my favor and instructed the jury to disregard, but the hidden question, *"Did Floyd hear the deputy arrive and ignore him?"* Had already been planted in the juror's minds and couldn't be removed by a simple command to disregard.

As the judge gave his ruling, the Prosecutor gave me a wry smile as if to say, "too late buddy I made my point."

"The Prosecutor's smile reminded me of the smiles I would sometimes get on the basketball court when an opponent would sneak a ball by me and make a basket. The prosecutor was playing a game. For him it seemed to be all about winning, not about truth or justice.

The prosecutor continued to question the Deputy.

"Did the man standing over the woman resist when you approached?"

"No, he collapsed."

"Was he unconscious?"

"Yes, he appeared to be

"Could he have been faking, pretending to be unconscious?"

I started to object on the same grounds, "calling for speculation", when the Prosecutor gave me another 'gotcha' smile and I decided to let the question go. The judge interrupted. He knew that I could, and should have, objected, but I waived off the opportunity. I reasoned that if I objected now and then brought up the prosecutor's question later in cross-examination, I would appear to be violating my own objection. If I could get the Deputy to dispute his own testimony, however, I would have a better chance of erasing the damage caused by doubts interjected by the Prosecutor.

The Prosecutor was using a courtroom trick to imply that Floyd was intentionally manipulating the situation at the crime scene by faking unconsciousness. I hated to admit that a courtroom, where an individual's fate was being determined, could become a game, but it had, and I had no choice but to play the game. I couldn't allow the prosecutor to gain an advantage using gaming techniques without responding.

The Prosecutor continued to question the Deputy, forcing him to describe the grizzly accounts of the assumed crime scene and introduced photographs of Floyd's grandmother laying on the ground and of the mutilated fawn, He also introduced portions of the deceased's clothing that had blood on them. When he finished I began my cross-examination.

"Deputy; what prompted you to go to the Brenner Farm on the morning of the incident?"

"I received a radio call from the dispatcher instructing me to respond to a 911 call."

I had to choose my words carefully. The prosecutor referred to the Brenner farm as; "the crime scene", and Melisa Brenner as; "the victim", as if Floyd's guilt was a given. He was leading the jury to a conclusion before the introduction of all the facts and was carefully presenting a sanitized version of the facts to match his foregone conclusions. He was playing the game well.

"Did the dispatcher give you any details about the 911 call?"

I had planned on entering the 911 call into evidence and playing it for the jury, but with the prosecutor busy twisting the facts, I felt the testimony from one of his own key witnesses would be a better counter to the slant he was putting on things.

"The dispatcher told me she had received a call from a hysterical man claiming that a tree had killed his grandmother."

"Did you question the dispatcher about the call? Did you think the call was strange?"

"We get a lot of strange calls so I didn't question her, I assumed there had been an accident involving a tree and asked her to send an ambulance."

I couldn't have hoped for a better response. The Deputy, who had just a moment ago described the situation at the farm as a crime scene, in response to the Prosecutor's carefully scripted questions, was now describing it as an accident.

"And when you arrived, and first saw Floyd standing over his grandmother, did you immediately change your mind and assume that it wasn't an accident? Is that why you called for backup and waited for the Sheriff?"

"No, I had no idea what had happened, but Mr. Brenner was acting like someone completely out of control and he is a big man. I thought it was a good idea to wait for help."

"Was the accused hurting or threatening the women you saw laying on the ground?"

"No, he was wailing and cursing something about a tree and was pulling at his beard."

"Did you see a tree nearby that he was cursing about?"

"The only tree I saw was near the house but there were no obvious marks and I couldn't tell if it was the tree he was screaming about."

"Did the defendant have any weapons in his hands or were any nearby?"

"No."

"Did the situation you encountered at the farm make any sense? Could you make an assessment or reach any immediate conclusions as to what had happened?"

"No."

So far so good, I was confident that I had dispelled at least some of the prosecutor's initial description of the incident as an obvious crime scene but I assumed he would call the Sheriff to the stand later to replay and reinforce his version of events. I concluding my cross-examination and returned to my seat.

Floyd looked concerned.

"Was I acting that crazy?" he whispered. "I think the jury believed the prosecutor. Why can't I just take the stand and tell them the truth?"

"Not a good idea," I answered in a low voice. "Until recently you couldn't remember much of what happened. The prosecutor will cross examine you and make you out to be a liar. He will also try to make you angry enough to say or do something that will convince the jury that you were capable of hurting your grandmother."

The next witness the prosecution called was a surprise. Somehow, the prosecution's investigators had found a witness to Floyd beating his piano into pieces.

"The prosecution calls Willard Stampel to the stand."

A bearded man with overalls and suspenders took the stand and was administered the oath. He was obviously a farmer and probably Amish.

"Mr. Stampel, Do you go to the Brenner Farm on occasion?"

"Yes I deliver hay and straw for their steers whenever they run low."

"In late April of this year did you make a delivery to the Brenner farm?"

"Yep, Floyd sent me a letter asking for forty bales each of straw and hay and I delivered it the next week."

"And when you arrived at the farm to make your delivery what did you see?"

"I saw Floyd out in the yard pounding on a piano with a big sledge hammer. It was pretty much destroyed"

"Did Floyd seem angry or upset?"

"He wasn't too friendly and he had a bad arm in a sling and some bruises so I helped him stack the bales in the barn and got my money and left."

"Did you talk to him? Did he tell you why he was destroying the piano?"

"No, he didn't seem like he was in the mood for talking so I took my money and left?"

The Prosecutor announced that he had no more questions for his surprise witness, gave me the 'gotcha' smile, and sat down.

The surprise witness caught me off guard. The Prosecutor was beginning to paint Floyd as a violent man and I was certain that his next witness would be the neighbor with whom Floyd had fought. I couldn't let the testimony of the Amish farmer slide and I couldn't be certain how he would answer my questions but I had to play the game.

I stalled as long as I could, trying to craft a few harmless questions that wouldn't evoke answers I didn't want, but I came up empty. I had no choice but to wing it.

"Mr. Stampel, did you think Floyd was destroying the piano because he was angry with it?"

I wasn't sure why I had asked the question but it was too late. All I could hope for was that he wouldn't say, "Yes".

"Nope," the witness answered, "I assumed he was beating it into small pieces to put in the trash."

I had been lucky and decided to try my luck one more time.

"Mr. Stampel, did Floyd tell you how he got bruised?"

"Yep, he said he tangled with his favorite bull and lost."

The jury laughed and the judge banged his gavel and called for order.

I announced I had no more questions for the witness, and as he stepped down, I returned the prosecutor's gotcha smile. I was right about the next witness being the neighbor Floyd had confronted, and I did my best to defuse his testimony by making him recount his own inflammatory remarks about Floyd's deceased father. It didn't go as well this time and I sensed the Jury might be buying into the picture the prosecution was painting of Floyd as an angry and potentially dangerous man. Floyd also noticed the jury's changing attitude and gave me a worried look.

"This is beginning to scare me." He said.

I spent a few minuets after court going over the day's proceedings with Floyd and tried to reassure him that things were going as well as could be expected. I gave Floyd a ride home, turned down his invitation to visit, and returned to my office to prepare for the next courtroom tug of war between innuendo and truth.

CHAPTER TWENTY

Floyd's first day in court was not what he expected. He returned to the safety of his apartment exhausted. Twelve strangers were determining his future and an aggressive and disagreeable prosecutor was doing his best to make certain that his future would be spent behind bars. I was fighting for him and Daphne had been there to support him, but as a member of the press, she was forced to stand in the back of the courtroom instead of sitting nearby.

Floyd needed her companionship. She helped him remain calm and made him feel human in a world that was sometimes, insane. Julia knew Floyd would be stressed after court and acting more like a mother than a landlady, she prepared a meal for him, knowing it would probably go to uneaten.

Floyd wanted to escape but there was nowhere to hide. The only things he could do to get the day's court proceedings out of his head were to paint or play the piano. The late afternoon sun was still filtering through the skylights in Julia's studio and Floyd took advantage of the warm yellow light to begin a new painting. Julia brought his meal and placed it beside the brush rack. She helped Floyd begin his painting by stretching a new canvas and offered advice on composition and color. As Floyd began to sketch his newest vision of the tree, Julia asked if she could review some of his completed works.

Floyd had been prolific in his experiments with oils and nearly a dozen finished paintings were stacked in the corner of the studio. Julia began to look through them and, was again impressed by his innate ability.

There was a special style to his work that made his paintings mesmerizing. All the paintings were of the tree but each painting was made unique by changing settings and changing emotions. The skies in the paintings varied from bright and sunny, to dark and stormy and the tree itself was depicted as warm and inviting in one painting, and rough and frightening in another. The composition of all the various depections was excellent and the use of shadow and color to express a variety of moods was remarkable. There was also an evident progression in Floyd's works. The enthusiasm and returning zest for life evident in his earlier paintings had transitioned to dark and foreboding in his latest works. Worn away by a flood of accusing words from the press, his paintings reflected a slow erosion of his mood but, in spite of Floyd's growing depression, dead animals or terrible image of his father impaled on the tree's limb, were never present. The tree took on its many moods without the need for gore.

"Floyd?" Julia held up one of his earlier paintings. "Have you ever thought about sharing these with others? They are very good and shouldn't go to waste hidden here in my studio."

Floyd stopped sketching and looked at the painting Julia was holding. Before he could reply, she continued.

"Without the farm being productive and without being able to do any masonry work you will run out of funds sooner or later. Your father's life insurance and the equity in the farm is a nice cushion but your medical and legal bills are adding up fast. I think your paintings are good enough to be displayed and sold. Would you consider selling them?"

"I don't paint to make money," Floyd replied, "and I don't think I like the idea of a lot of strangers staring at them. The paintings come out of a part of my brain I can't control and they open a hole into my soul that I don't want people to look into. I'm already accused of being a monster. If people start judging my paintings, they might also see me as a madman. I don't think it's a good idea."

"I think you're wrong." Julia replied. "I think they will see a great talent and begin to understand the tragedy that surrounds the tree and you. I think they will feel your pain and see your forgiveness. I think they will learn from your paintings that all of us have the power to control our own destiny by adjusting our view of the world around us. Your paintings show a shining vision sliding into darkness, something we have all experienced. I know it won't be easy but if you can begin to find your way back, your paintings will begin to show the resiliency that exists in every human spirit, a resiliency that can bring us back into the light. It would be a wonderful gift. Think about it."

Julia's doorbell rang just as she finished her speech. She handed the painting she was holding to Floyd and left to answer the door.

It was Daphne. She had been in the courtroom and had seen Floyd lower his head as the prosecutor made him out to be an angry out of control individual without a conscience. She had finished recording her latest newscast and was worried about Floyd and wanted to see him. She wanted to be near him and her empathy made her realize that she was indeed, falling in love.

"I tried the bell to Floyd's apartment," Daphne said, "but he didn't answer. Is he here?

Julia let Daphne in and motioned toward the studio.

"He seems depressed," Julia said. "I'm worried about him and he refuses to eat. We just had a talk about showing his paintings and I hope he agrees. I have a friend with a gallery in New York that I am certain would be interested Why don't you wait here for a minute while I get something from the wine cellar, maybe you can cheer him up."

Julia returned with a bottle of Bordeaux, a corkscrew and two glasses. Daphne took the wine and entered the studio. She expected to find Floyd engrossed in his painting, instead he was setting on a small bench with his mask and gloves next to him. He was holding the painting that Julia had just reviewed.

"Are you ok?" Daphne asked.

Floyd turned away and reached for his mask.

"Don't put it on, I've seen your scars before, they don't offend me."

"They offend me", Floyd answered, and slipped the elastic band of his mask over his head.

"When I talk to people without my mask I can tell they try not look at the scars or my bad eye. It's obvious they're focusing on only half of my face so they won't embarrass me. With the mask on, they look at me without being self-conscious. The plastic surgery is helping but until I look normal, I need the mask. It protects me from the curious and lets me talk to my friends without the scars getting in the way. I'm not proud of my scars, especially since I caused them."

"You didn't cause your injuries," Daphne responded, "They were an accident."

"Maybe," Floyd answered, "Maybe not. That's what my trial is all about. If you hurt someone when you're drunk, you're responsible. If you hurt someone when you're sleep walking, is it the same?"

"I don't know," Daphne said as she struggled with the corkscrew, "but I know you are a good man and that you didn't intentionally hurt your grandmother. You didn't know she was chasing you. You didn't even know she was there until you saw her fall, and then you tried to help her."

Floyd stood up and took the wine and cork screw from Daphne, and finished opening the bottle.

"I saw you standing in the back of the court room." Floyd began, "Thank you for being there."

Daphne sat down next to Floyd, took the open bottle, handed him a glass, and steadied his hand as she poured his wine. She felt sorry for Floyd and his impossible situation. She was convinced that the prosecutor was pushing for an indictment because of the notoriety surrounding the case. He was trying to make a name for himself at Floyd's expense.

Daphne continued to console Floyd, and as they sipped the wine, the sun slipped below the horizon and the studio became a magical place, filled with moonlight. As the light faded, the wine took effect and their moods changed. Daphne's compassion drifted into passion and Floyd began to relax. Daphne moved closer to Floyd and kissed him. At first, Floyd drew away. He had avoided intimacy all of his adult life, but the desire in Daphne's eyes drew him back. They kissed again and climbed the stairs to Floyd's bedroom.

Daphne stayed with Floyd in his apartment over night and the next morning Floyd seemed confused, but in a much better mood.

As the sun rose, Floyd made a decision regarding his paintings. He told Daphne of his decision and that he was anxious to tell Julia that he would allow them to be shown. Daphne kissed him as she left and told him she approved of his decision.

The night with Floyd had convinced Daphne that her love for Floyd was real. It also made her realize that she was making a commitment to a man who might be spending years in jail.

Floyd showered and dressed. After his first intimacy, he was a bit more conscious of his appearance and took the time to trim his beard. The judge had ordered a continuance until after Floyd's next reconstructive surgery and the procedure would give him a few days free. He was anxious to return to his paintings and anxious to talk to Julia but knew Julia liked to sleep late and hesitated before going downstairs.

While Floyd waited for Julia to begin her day, he called me to find out if showing his paintings would hurt his court case. I didn't think a small art showing would detract from his defense and a little positive local notoriety might help. I had no idea that Julia was planning a showing in a prestigious New York gallery.

When Floyd could wait no longer, he phoned Julia to be certain she was awake. Julia answered and asked him to come down for coffee. When Floyd arrived in Julia's kitchen, she had breakfast waiting.

"I was going to call you," Julia said. "I found the food from last night uneaten and the wine bottle empty and thought you might be hungry this morning. Did you think about my suggestion to show your paintings?"

"Yes," Floyd answered. "It seems like a good idea. I just hope I'm not embarrassed. I asked my lawyer what he thought because I was afraid it might screw things up with the trial, but he said it would be ok. Are you sure they should be shown? I like painting but my tree paintings don't seem good enough for an art gallery. Do you think anyone will want to buy them?"

"You have three things going for you." Julia answered, "Your paintings are good, very good, the tree is famous, and your name is already well known. Like it or not, you are already a celebrity. You have a natural talent and you might as well take advantage of being in the middle of a controversy. Circumstances beyond your control put you into this mess and the best thing you can do is give the mess a new direction, one that can benefit you. Showing your paintings will let others see things through your eyes. A good showing might also erase a lot of the damage done by bad press. I am delighted with your decision."

"But I can only paint the tree." Floyd responded. "Whenever I look at a blank canvas, the tree is all I see. I can't paint anything else."

"The tree is the universal subject in all of your paintings," Julia offered, "but each painting is unique. It is the same tree but it is different in every painting. Each painting expresses a different emotion. It is always in a different place on the canvas, the seasons reflected in the background vary and your eye is drawn to a different aspect of the tree in every one of your works. In one painting, you see the twisted vine in more detail, in another the knurled roots. Sometimes the tree is placid, sometimes peaceful and sometimes it is angry. The variety of emotions the tree expresses is as special as the art you bring to the canvas."

"I hope you're right, I really don't want to be embarrassed."

As soon as Floyd had finished his breakfast, Julia called her friend Douglas in New York.

"Douglas, this is Julia in Ohio, I have come across a special talent worthy of an exhibition in your gallery. I would love it if you would take the time to look at a few of his paintings and see if you agree. His very first oil had a masterpiece quality and my guess is that he is a savant. He paints only one subject but portrays it differently in every painting. The collection now stands at about two dozen but he is very prolific and produces several paintings a week. You may have heard of the Floyd Brenner trial and the famous tree. Floyd is living with me while he is on trial and is using my studio to turn out modern masterpieces at an unbelievable rate."

"It's good to hear from you too Julia. You must be excited about these paintings, you didn't even bother to say hello. How are you?"

"I'm sorry Douglas that was rude of me, I'm doing well, how are you doing?"

"I am well, thanks. You have very good timing. I will be removing my latest showing next week and have nothing to replace it. I haven't seen you in a few years. Would you mind a personal visit? I could review Floyd's work and we could get reacquainted?"

Julia was so excited she stood on her tiptoes. When she hung up the phone, she clapped her hands together like a teenager that had just been asked to the prom.

Floyd was happy for her, but still doubtful. His compulsion to paint was not from a desire for recognition. It came from the same dark place that had driven him to the unconscious acts that resulted in his grandmother's death. Grandma had forgiven him from beyond the grave, but society hadn't made up its mind.

CHAPTER TWENTY-ONE

After the Governor's reprimand, Dr. Brice intensified his efforts. If the Governor was successful in shutting him down, his investigations would be cut short, and a scientific find that could affect many disciplines would be lost. Fortunately, the geneticist from Washington had convinced a member of the House of Representatives to convene a subcommittee to hear their findings and determine if federal protection of the tree was warranted. It was a hastily assembled committee assigned the sole purpose of hearing testimony related to the importance of the unique plant and its value as a source of scientific information. If Dr. Brice were to insure further access to the tree, he would have to convince the committee that further study would provide new and valuable information for genetics, symbiotic relationships, and longevity in plants, but he was under a serious time constraint.

Further physical examinations of the tree's anatomical features were unlikely to produce anything that would convince a group of politicians that the tree should be protected, or that further studies were warranted. Instead of more gross-feature examinations, Dr. Brice concentrated on trying to determine the tree's age and unravel its genetic code. It was a daunting task. The tree's genome contained ninety eighty chromosomes and hundreds of thousands of alleles. Some of the sequencing was familiar but there were so many strands of DNA to analyze that Dr. Brice had to recruit a small army of graduate students from many universities to help. Coordinating the many findings from his expanded team was difficult and he worried that nothing of real significance would be found in time. Then, a female graduate student, working in Dr. Brice's own lab, caught something that had been missed.

Wendy's area of study was criminal genetics. After graduation, she hoped to work as a genetic pathologist for one of the larger crime labs. What she noticed in the tree's genome were markers. The markers were similar to those crime labs insert into DNA to identify evidence samples.

Dr. Brice wanted to know more and called Wendy.

"What I noticed," Wendy explained, "are sequences in several genomes that resemble the markers crime labs are now inserting into DNA evidence samples to avoid misidentifying the samples. With a distinct marker inserted, samples can't be switched or applied to the wrong criminal case. The markers are constructed allele sequences that stand out as artificial.

"And you think you have found markers in the tree's DNA that are artificial, is that correct?"

"Yes." Wendy answered. "There are about a hundred markers in a long sequence that repeats often in the same chromosome."

"To be universally distributed throughout every cell in the tree," Wendy continued, "the markers either had to be natural, or had to have been inserted into the trees DNA before it started to grow. They had to be in the seed of the tree before it germinated or in a graft from a previous plant."

At first, Dr. Brice was skeptical, but after rechecking the graduate student's results, he had to agree that the strange codon placements seemed to be markers and the same markers showed up in the exact same chromosome. Dr. Brice immediately set up a teleconference for his entire research team.

With everyone on line, he briefed his team.

"One of our researchers has identified a sequence of alleles that appear to be artificial inserts in the genetic material of the Tree. We have confirmed her findings but have no idea if they are significant. Wendy will give you the location of the markers and I would like everyone to concentrate on trying to see if they are significant, and if so, why, and if they mean anything."

After the teleconference ended and the entire team was on a new quest, Dr. Brice questioned Wendy further.

"Do you have a preliminary explanation for the markers? You do realize your working with the DNA of an ancient plant?"

Wendy remained quiet. Was Dr. Brice asking a serious question or doubting findings he had already confirmed?

"Yes sir, I understand where the samples came from but these codons are definitely being used as markers, and in my opinion appear to have been intentionally inserted. If you know the age of the plant you might be able to tell when they were inserted, but not why."

"The plant is definitely older than the discovery of cellular structures." Dr. Brice responded. "Hell, this plant may have been here before man became human. Something is off. Either the radio carbon dating of the minerals trapped in the plant when it was a sapling is wrong or these supposed markers are a natural occurring arrangement."

"They are not natural", Wendy replied. "Normal codons don't work like that. They look like intentionally inserted markers".

Dr. Brice was looking for a reason to save the tree but not this. He began to pace back and forth behind his desk.

"I will never be able to convince anyone that the DNA was manipulated in the tree before Man discovered fire. Are you certain these are intentionally inserted?"

Wendy was adamant. "Yes, in my opinion they are artificial and were intentionally inserted".

Dr. Brice ended the call with his student and sat alone at his desk for several hours. Maybe the Governor was right. It was all too improbable. Maybe he was just kicking up dust, or maybe the markers were in the dust or in some of the animal tissue the tree had ingested. Modern investigations were turning up other examples of strange transfers of genetic material, including DNA from fetal sons in the brains of their mothers. If DNA from fetal cells could transfer from a fetus to its mother during pregnancy by penetrating the body brain barrier, maybe it could transfer in other ways as well.

Dr. Brice rushed to setup another conference call to switch the focus of his team a second time, but before he could redirect their efforts, another of his assistants asked him to look at one of the lab's computer monitors. On the monitor was a researcher from one of the teams in Canada. The Canadian researcher was pointing at a printout of the DNA marker sequence.

"I was studying Wendy's markers when I noticed a somewhat regular pattern of alleles between the markers. When I looked closer, I spotted something very strange. There are twenty-six sequences between the markers that repeat over and over. The sequences are irregular and I don't know what they are, but for symmetry to repeat this many times isn't natural".

The tree was now revealing secrets hidden in its DNA that were both unbelievable and undecipherable.

"What the hell is going on?" Dr. Brice shouted.

"Someone figure out what those sequences mean".

For the rest of the day, half of Dr. Brice's volunteers worked on deciphering the tree's repetitive alleles, while the other half dug deeper into adjacent chromosomes looking for other hidden patterns. After many hours and many discussions, the team was at a dead end and gave up. Wendy, however, was not willing to quit and took home a copy of the marker sequences.

By chance, Wendy's roommate, a math major, saw the DNA graph on Wendy's desk. "That's interesting", the roommate commented, "what is it?"

"It's a puzzle." Wendy replied, and unfolded the rest of the long graph letting it spill off her desk onto the floor.

Wendy's roommate got down on her knees and began counting the dark marks between the lighter marks. "These are prime numbers", she said casually, "Is this some sort of computer experiment?"

"Oh my God", Wendy screamed, "Are you sure?"

"Yes I'm sure," The roommate responded, "Look, they start with two, three, five, seven, eleven, and go all the way to one hundred and one. Why are you so excited?"

"You have just decoded our first alien contact." Wendy screamed and danced around the room.

"We aren't alone and you just proved it".

Wendy scooped up the graph and ran out the door. The realization that a complex mathematical concept had been placed in the DNA of a plant before the advent of modern humans was more than an interesting scientific find, it was evidence that intelligent life existed before man. The implications were so immense that if one believed the message, it would confirm some of the myths surrounding the tree. Finding evidence of an older and possibly wiser form of life than Man was certain to have profound effects.

Wendy immediately contacted Dr. Brice.

"Dr. Brice we have an answer, and it is a blockbuster. In between the markers, a particular amino acid is being used as a counter and it is counting prime numbers.

There is no mistaking the sequence, and prime numbers are a mathematical construct, not something that occurs naturally. An intelligent species with advanced mathematical knowledge and advanced biological skills left a message in the tree."

Dr. Brice reviewed the evidence repeatedly. Deep down he wanted to refute the findings but he couldn't. He had no choice but to proceed and in just a few days the congressional committee charged with evaluating the tree's scientific value would convene.

Convincing politicians that a rare plant needed protection would be difficult enough. Convincing them that aliens were involved would be impossible.

CHAPTER TWENTY-TWO

The meeting began with a reading into the record of the purpose of the committee and the names of those in attendance. The Chairman called upon Dr. Brice to give a short description and history of the tree, the tree's physical aspects, its location and some of the myths surrounding it. Dr. Brice described how a snowmobile accident had precipitated a series of events that made the tree the focus of media attention and why he had been brought in to examine it.

"The tree is now covered with a giant inflatable bubble," Dr. Brice continued. "Teams of investigators are delving into the trees origin, age, and genetics. If it were an ordinary plant I wouldn't be here and the tree would have been forgotten, but it is not an ordinary plant. The tree is a union of two plants that share their genetic language in a way that we haven't seen before, and their unusual relationship has given them both an extremely long life. The pair could be one the oldest living multi cellular things on earth, much older than the oldest redwood or banyan tree. The symbiotic pair of plants is also able to generate living energy through both photosynthesis and by metabolizing animal proteins. All of these things make the tree an important scientific find and because it is a living thing, and not an inanimate object, its preservation and protection is essential."

Dr Brice hesitated for a moment before making his next point. What he was about to reveal was difficult to believe. If the members of the committee took him seriously, the tree would become one of the most important objects on Earth. If they didn't take him seriously, he would be discredited and a great treasure would be lost.

He took a deep breath, he wasn't certain he even believed in what he was about to reveal, but it was his best hope to save the tree.

"What I am about to tell you I didn't believe at first. When I first saw the results I thought we were imagining things and to be absolutely certain I had the results checked by many labs."

"First let me bring you up to speed on where we are in the science of genetics. We're using genetics to trace evolutionary histories, to clone animals, alter plants, cause goats to produce liquid spider silk in their milk, and have even resurrected an extinct relative of the cow by placing the genes of the extinct animal into a cow's egg. If it were ethical, we could probably clone humans. We use genetics to solve crimes, cure diseases and forecast vulnerabilities to future health problems. We can also alter genetic codes and insert markers to insure we don't mistake one gene sample from another and, if we can manipulate genetic material and insert markers so can others, and this is the hard part to swallow."

"We have found intentionally inserted markers in the DNA of this unique plant that were not inserted by humans. The tree's DNA appears to have been intentionally altered long before humans became civilized."

Several of the committee members, including the chairperson, raised their eyebrows and leaned back in their chairs. Dr. Brice ignored the obvious switch from curiosity to caution and continued.

"When we examined the genetic makeup of the tree we found it to have a combined chromosome count of ninety eight. This isn't unusual. Humans have forty-six separate strands of DNA in the nucleus of each of their cells, and some plants have over one thousand. There are thousands of alleles, individual pieces of DNA, in each chromosome so there are many places to place markers and splice in new sequences. The first unusual sequence of DNA we found in the tree was between markers. We tried to dismiss the regularity as a natural occurrence but then we discovered that a long strand of DNA in one of the tree's chromosomes was repeating. The unusual sequence began with two identical alleles followed by a marker followed by three identical alleles another marker then five, seven, eleven, thirteen, and so on. For those of you that are mathematicians these are prime numbers, numbers that can only be divided by one and itself. The list of all prime numbers is endless, the list in the trees chromosome consists of twenty-six primes from two to one hundred and one and the prime number list is repeated several times. There is no way that a list of the first twenty six prime numbers could have been an accident of nature, especially when it is repeated."

The committee chairperson stopped Dr Brice from going any further.

"And why would anyone go to the trouble of splicing in bits of DNA to match prime numbers? And how did they get it into the tree? You're right Dr. Brice this is indeed difficult to believe."

Dr. Brice closed his eyes. The Chairman's next statement could bury the tree and end his career but before the Chairman could finish another member of the committee spoke up.

"Dr Brice, before we go any further with what is about to turn into science fiction, could one of your associates have created this genetic pattern and implanted it or altered your samples?"

"No, many independent researchers have sampled and tested the results and the results are always the same."

"And why would prime numbers show up in a tree's DNA? Does Nature have a penchant for mathematics, is God trying to tell us something, or is someone playing a trick?"

"I don't know about God," Dr. Brice replied, "but someone or something definitely inserted a rational concept into the DNA of the tree. It didn't happen by accident."

Another member of the committee joined the conversation.

"Could this miracle insertion of numbers have been inserted recently, in the past few years? Could the tree be much younger than you think?"

"For every cell in the tree, including its sap, to incorporate the prime number pattern it would have to have been inserted into the DNA of the tree's seed before germination and the tree predates our discovery of genetics by tens of thousands of years. Particle samples of minerals trapped inside the tree during its early growth have been carbon dated at over fifty thousand years."

"I know this all sounds bizarre." Dr. Brice continued. "It seems impossible, but the facts have been tested and verified. I'm trying to wrap my mind around the findings just as you are and that is exactly why we are here. Finding a message encoded in ancient DNA is like finding an ancient scroll written before man invented language. We need to understand why the message was inserted and what it means. We can't ignore this discovery. We need to understand why the tree's genes were manipulated, how it was done, when it was done, and who did it. We also need to look for other messages. The tree appears to be a one of a kind life form. Understanding the message in the tree, and using the information wisely demands that we protect the tree. What the tree may reveal I can't predict but to ignore it, or worse, destroy it, would be unconscionable."

The committee room remained quiet. The politicians, usually driven by a compulsion to talk first and think later, had been rendered mute. They all knew they needed to reflect before speaking. The idea of a mathematical message hidden in the microscopic cells of a tree had serious implications, not only for science, but also for their political careers. The committee chairperson asked Dr. Brice to leave the room while the committee considered his request.

With Dr. Brice waiting outside, and the door closed, the chairman addressed the other members of the committee.

"I'm afraid we were just handed a double edged sword with no handle. If the genetic number thing is proven a hoax and we associate ourselves with it, we will appear fools. If proven true and we ignore it, we will look equally foolish. This alien message in a tree idea is political poison."

The decision by the politicians was unanimous. None of the committee members, no matter how curious, was willing to risk associating themselves with the concept, and after calling Dr. Brice back into the room; the committee chairperson announced their decision.

"Your argument is well presented but you have only one option available to continue protecting the tree and that is to extend the quarantine. As a congressional committee of inquiry, we don't have the authority to do what you ask. Only the Center for Disease Control or the Environmental Protection Agency can impose quarantine. We therefore suggest that you take your request to the CDC or the EPA. The CDC will be looking for evidence that the tree, if left unprotected, could present a general health hazard and I doubt that your very convincing argument of a hidden message in the tree's DNA will sway them. The EPA will be looking for evidence that the tree presents a hazard to other plants or wild life. When you ask for quarantine you should bring evidence that the tree presents either an environmental hazard or a health hazard."

Having sidestepped the awkward need to acknowledge or deny a message hidden in the DNA of a tree the committee members unanimously agreed to adjourn.

Politics had been played to perfection. The committee had transferred their dilemma from a congressional concern to unsuspecting bureaucrats in the executive branch. The true implications of a discovery that pointed to an ancient intelligent intervention seemed lost on the members of the committee. They focused only on protecting their public image and swept aside the discovery as interesting but irrelevant, and happily returned to the House of Representatives to deal with safer and more mundane matters.

CHAPTER TWENTY-THREE

Dr Brice was discouraged by the reaction of the congressional committee but was unwilling to give up. He returned to the investigation of the tree, but was no longer searching for additional meaning in the DNA message.

He needed a new argument if he was going to save the tree, and turned his attention to finding evidence that the tree posed a threat to the humans. He knew that any evidence he might present to the CDC could also be a double-edged sword. If the tree presented a real danger to humans, the CDC could easily recommend that it be destroyed regardless of the trees scientific importance.

He couldn't fabricate evidence or lie about his findings. All he could do was redirect his inquiry to see if the tree presented any threats warranting quarantine.

Dr. Brice had visited the tree before it was covered. He had seen the chain saw stuck deep into its trunk and noticed the metal of the saw eaten away by the tree's acidic sap. He saw the mummified doe lying on the roots of the tree and thought he saw the roots move. He had also seen the bandages on Floyd's face and hands and thought of Daphne.

When Daphne needed an assessment of the tree to protect Floyd, she called Dr. Brice. Now, Dr. Brice needed an assessment of Floyd to protect the tree and he called Daphne.

"It's nice to hear from you Dr. Brice. How is the research going?"

"It's going well, but we've hit a snag and I could use your help"

"What can I do?" Daphne answered.

"I need medical access to examine Floyd's burns plus blood tests and tissue samples. I'm looking for any infections that might have been caused by contact with the tree. The Governor wants the tree destroyed and all research stopped. He is afraid our findings will embarrass him and make Ohio look bad. Our only hope in saving the tree and continuing our study is to get the Feds to replace the Ohio quarantine with a Federal quarantine. We need to show the CDC that the tree can be either dangerous or valuable or both and I'm having trouble with the valuable part."

"It sounds like a hell of a tight rope your walking." Daphne replied. "How is examining Floyd going to help?"

"I'm not sure."

"Other than the tree's nasty sap I have no idea what I am looking for but you can help by checking to see if Floyd has developed any physical or behavioral symptoms since the incident.

Daphne thought for a moment.

"I can put you in touch with the emergency room doctor who treated Floyd in the hospital. Would that help?"

"It would be a start, how soon can you arrange a meeting, I'm under a real time constraint. I need to get ahead of the Governor before he sends the National Guard in with flame throwers and burns what might be our first alien contact."

Daphne's reporter instincts instantly went on full alert.

"What did you just say?

"Is the tree alien?"

Dr Brice had opened Pandora's Box with a slip of the tongue and Daphne was not about to let it go. Dr. Brice hesitated for a moment and then decided to let the secret go public.

"You might as well know, in fact, some spectacular press might work in our favor."

"What we have found in the trees genetic strands is astounding. There are unusual genetics associated with the way the tree and its companion vine share genes, but we have also discovered evidence that some of its genes have been altered, and a repeating genetic code inserted. Repeating genetic codes are common in nature. All plants and animals have long strands of repeating alleles that are like stuttering and seem to have no purpose, but the repeating codes we found in the tree represent a mathematical concept. The imbedded mathematical sequence could only have been inserted purposely by intelligent beings familiar with both mathematics and genetics. The repeating genetic strands we discovered were a list of prime numbers from two up to one hundred and one, and just to be certain the sequence was understood as an intentional insertion, the sequence was marked and repeated several times."

"Are you certain about this?" Daphne interrupted.

"I am absolutely certain." Dr. Brice answered. "The genetic message is encoded in every cell of the tree, and unless acquired by some unknown method, had to be inserted by manipulating genes in the seed or the mother plant that produced the seed. The tree is very old and the message has to be at least as old as the tree. It is definitely much older than our discovery of prime numbers. Either way we have found an intelligent message from the past that predates modern man."

Daphne was stunned. Unlike the politicians and the Governor, she understood the importance of Dr. Brice's discovery. As a student of history, she knew that human's had been inventing gods and postulating intelligent aliens since the beginning of human awareness. Now, they had found proof, but they didn't find it where they expected.

They didn't find it on top of a mountain or another planet, or in a radio message from space, instead, they found it hidden in the microscopic strands of a tree's DNA.

"This is huge." Daphne exclaimed. Have you checked your data?"

"Yes," Dr Brice answered," we have repeated the tests many times. The prime number sequence is always there. How you interpret the whole thing is what matters, and we don't have a good interpretation. We looked for more messages but so far, all we have found is a short tweet from an unknown sender sent sometime in the distant past saying; *we were here* and we are smart enough to leave a universal mathematical concept in a digital biological format. It seems that another intelligent life form has said 'hello' in a way we never expected."

Daphne was in shock. All journalists dream of getting the scoop of the year but this was the biggest scoop in human history.

"This is so big I don't know quite how to deal with it." Daphne replied.

"Letting the world know that another intelligent life form has contacted us will change everything, but

I doubt if I will be able to get anyone to believe me. If the tabloids get hold of the story their reputation for sensationalism, combined with the gullibility of their readers, could also turn the most important discovery in the history of mankind into comic book science."

Daphne hesitated before responding further.

"If this is real the importance of your discovery has to be assimilated slowly and will need confirmation by scientists throughout the world."

"You're right." Dr. Brice answered. "Even if the antennas of SETE suddenly receive a message from space it would instantly be challenged. Proof of extraterrestrial life, especially intelligent life, will trigger defensive reactions by every religion in the world, will affect most scientific disciplines, change international relationships, and force everyone to adjust their self-image. In one way or another, all of us depend upon a common belief that we are unique and exclusive. To find out that we are not, that we are not alone, and that we may not be the most advanced life form in the universe, will deal a serious blow to our collective egos."

CHAPTER TWENTY-FOUR

The grand jury reconvened and I was back in court before I was ready. I had heard nothing from Daphne and had no idea that Dr. Brice's team had discovered something that would blow the case against Floyd apart.

Daphne and Brice's team had done a good job of keeping the lid on the DNA message and members of congress were treating it as a poison pill. One of the most important finds in the history of mankind was being withheld from the world because of its' potential impact.

Daphne arrived at the courthouse late. The proceedings had begun and she was forced to find a place at the side of the room. Whenever I looked in her direction, she signaled that she needed to talk to me but I had to concentrate on the trial. The prosecutor had put the Coroner on the stand and had him relate his findings regarding healed fractures in Floyd's Grandmother's arms. He intimated they could have been the result of earlier abuse. I countered by having the Coroner testify that the elder Brenner suffered from a degenerative bone disease and that the small fractures could have resulted from everyday stresses. I also had him testify that he had determined the cause of death as a heart attack.

The prosecutor's next witness was another surprise. He called Floyd's accountant to the stand and I assumed he was going to expose the misuse of farm subsidies or maybe tax evasion. His first question told me otherwise.

"You are the Brenner's accountant", is that correct?

The accountant answered in the affirmative.

"And did you attend social events at the Brenner farm?"

Again, the answer was "Yes".

"Please describe those events for the jury."

The accountant gave a brief description of Floyd's annual pig roasts. The prosecutor then asked if the witness observed Floyd drinking during the events.

Again, the answer was "Yes."

The prosecutor pushed further.

"And did the defendant get drunk at these pig roasts?"

The accountant hesitated.

"You were there." The prosecutor continued. Was alcohol served, and did you observe Mr. Brenner getting drunk?"

I didn't like the line of questioning. I stood up and objected on the grounds that the question required a speculative answer and without a breathalyzer test given at the time, a casual observer couldn't make a reasonable evaluation. The judge overruled my objection and instructed the accountant to answer.

"Maybe he got a little drunk," the accountant answered, "but it was only beer and he was just enjoying his own party."

The prosecutor had succeeded in damaging Floyd's credibility but he wanted more and doubled down on the accountant's testimony using his favorite trick, innuendo.

"Have you seen Mr. Brenner drinking at home or in public on other occasions?"

I objected again, this time on the grounds that unless the witness could recount frequent observations of Floyd actually being under the influence of alcohol, that having a drink or two at ones own party was not evidence of substance abuse. The judge agreed with me, but it was too late, and I got another gotcha smile.

When I stood up to cross-examine the accountant, Daphne caught my attention again. She was holding her hands in a time out signal and mouthing the word "Tree". Unfortunately, Daphne's gestures attracted the attention of both the prosecutor and the judge. The prosecutor immediately held his hands out with palms up like a coach questioning a referee's call. The judge tapped his gavel lightly and admonished Daphne. She calmly reached in her purse, pulled out the promissory spoon, and held at her side where I could see it. I had no idea what she was trying to tell me.

I had to proceed.

I intended to debunk the prosecutor's scenario that Floyd was a frequent drinker, had caused his grandmother's death while in a drunken state, and then conveniently passed out when the police arrived.

I wanted the accountant to give a more complete picture of Floyd's behavior at his roasts. Then, if I needed more evidence of Floyd's sobriety, I could introduce hospital records or testimony from Floyd's Doctor, but Daphne's distraction made me focus on the tree and I had the perfect witness on the stand.

Floyd's accountant and his wife were regulars at the roasts and they always took the hayride that went past the tree. I knew the accountant and addressed him by name.

"Fred, what alcoholic beverages were served at Floyd's pig roasts?"

"Just a keg of beer," he answered.

"And did you ever observe Mr. Brenner consuming an excessive amount?"

"No."

"Did you participate in the hayride that Floyd provided?"

"Yes, my wife liked the hayride because it was a tour of the Brenner farm and always went past Floyd's tree."

The prosecutor objected, wondering where my line of questioning was going. He didn't want the now famous tree to become a distraction. I had the opposite objective and was certain that most or all of the jury had heard of the tree. It was continually making news and needed to be introduced in court as the reason both Floyd and his grandmother were in the field near the tree when his grandmother collapsed. I answered the prosecutor's objection by pointing out that the tree was central to what Floyd was doing when his grandmother died. The judge ruled in my favor and I continued.

"Why did Floyd take his guests past that particular tree on his hayrides, and what made the tree of interest to your wife?"

The prosecutor objected again but was overruled.

"Everyone liked going around the tree because it was really weird looking and Floyd would tell mythical stories about it that were fun and entertaining."

"And where on the farm was this tree located, in a grove of trees or near a road?"

"No, it was near the middle of the farm and stood by itself. The only things around it were open fields."

"Did Floyd drive the tractor that pulled the hay wagon on these tours?"

"Yes."

"And did he appear drunk as he drove or did he slur his speech as he told stories about the tree?"

"No, not at all"

Having rebuffed the drunk and dangerous innuendo, and having successfully introduced the tree into testimony, I excused the witness and asked that the facts surrounding Floyd's Father's death be entered into evidence. The prosecutor could hardly object to facts already known and made no objection.

I originally wanted to keep Floyd off the stand, but with the death of Floyd's father introduced, I switched strategies hoping the prosecutor would call Floyd, and he did.

Floyd took the stand and the prosecutor's first question made it clear what he was trying to do. He wanted to get

Floyd to contradicting himself and if possible make him angry.

"Floyd," he began. "You lived with your grandmother in the old farm house, is that correct?"

"Yes, I moved in with her just after she had a …" The prosecutor interrupted Floyd in mid sentence and in a loud voice directed him to answer with a simple "yes" or "no"

"Yes", Floyd repeated.

"Did you and your grandmother ever argue?"

"Only over petty things like….." Again, the prosecutor interrupted Floyd and directed him to answer with "yes or "no" only. Then the prosecutor began a speech.

"Small arguments can add up to stronger hostilities. Was that the case in …?"

I interrupted the prosecutor before he could finish his remarks.

"Your Honor, the prosecutor is making a statement, not asking a valid question. If he wants to know how

Floyd felt about his grandmother he should ask, not insinuate."

The judge directed the prosecutor to be more direct in his questioning and told him to continue. With his advantage lost in his attempt to confuse both the witness and the jury, he returned to his efforts to portray Floyd as an angry man that lacked control.

"Floyd, you got into a fight with one of your neighbors shortly before your grandmother met her unfortunate demise. Is that correct?"

"Yes, he was saying some terrible …" YES or NO the prosecutor shouted. This time he overdid his objection and his loud shout made some of the members of the jury flinch.

So far, he hadn't been able to make Floyd angry. Instead, he was aggravating the jury.

"And you destroyed your piano with a sledge hammer, yes or no?"

"Yes but…" Floyd caught himself and stopped but the jury got the point that there was more to the story than a simple yes or no.

"And you tried to cut down the tree you told stories about with a chain saw, yes or no?" Before Floyd could answer, the prosecutor continued his rant. "In fact you have a history of angry behavior, isn't that true?"

I stood up immediately and objected. Out of the corner of my eye, I could see members of the jury smiling in approval. The judge upheld my objection by admonishing the prosecutor and with his advantage lost, he announced that he had no more questions and sat down.

I approached the stand slowly. The prosecutor had put on a show intended to stir up strong emotions and had succeeded. I wanted to arouse empathy instead of anger and asked Floyd, in a soft voice that the jury could hear, if he was all right and if he could continue? Floyd nodded in the affirmative and looked down at his feet as if he had somehow played into the prosecution's hands. His cowering puppy reaction to the prosecutor was to my advantage but now I needed him to sit erect and answer my questions with authority so the jury could see and feel the truth in his answers.

"Floyd," I began in a gentle but commanding voice, "I want you to sit up straight and answer my questions fully. You don't have to stop at yes or no. We need to know what really happened the day your grandmother died. We know you don't have all the answers, but you can help us get to the truth by recounting what you do know, so try to relax and remember as many details as you can. I know it's difficult to recall some of the terrible things that led up to your grandmother's death, but we need to go over them to get at the truth."

"Who discovered your father after his accident?"

Floyd began cautiously.

"When we realized Dad hadn't come home that night I went looking for him. I found him stuck on a limb of the tree. The snow was heavy that night and I should have stopped him but I didn't. The snowmobile was wrecked and I tried to get him down but the limb was stuck through his chest and I couldn't pull him off. I had to wait for the ambulance and we had to pull the hay wagon out next to the tree and stand on it to reach him."

"After your father's accident did you continue to live with your grandmother?"

"Yes, my mother went to stay with my aunt at first and then went to a retreat home and I didn't want to be alone. Grandma felt the same way so we stayed together."

"Was your grandmother angry with you about not stopping your father from taking the snowmobile that night?"

"No, she knew he had insisted on taking the snowmobile in spite of my objections and she knew it was an accident."

"How did you feel about not stopping your father from driving across the farm in a bad snow storm?"

"I felt terrible, I still feel guilty. I feel like it was my fault."

"Before your father had his accident, you told stories about the tree. Where did those stories come from?"

"My father and my grandfather told me the stories."

"You have gloves on your hands and a mask on your face, why?

"I tried to cut the tree down and the sap from the tree burned me."

I asked Floyd to remove his mask. I wanted the jury to see his scars and realize that Floyd was telling the truth. At first, Floyd was reluctant but he finally gave-in and removed his mask. The jury was seated to his left and could see his damaged face and eye clearly. The female jurists covered their mouths with their hands and turned away. The male jurists were equally affected. I had connected Floyd to the tragedies of both his father's and his grandmother's deaths in a way the jury couldn't forget. Now I needed to have them hear Floyd's account of the events that resulted in his grandmother's death and led him through his recollections. I was careful to keep him on track and to prompt an explanation for his lapse of memory.

When Floyd had finished, he put his mask back on and left the witness stand. Floyd had done well but I expected the prosecutor to recall him and try to trick him into contradicting himself.

Instead, the prosecutor surprised me and called Daphne to the stand.

Daphne was equally surprised, but composed herself and made her way from the side of the courtroom to the witness stand.

"Daphne you are a journalist, is that correct?"

Daphne gave a full account of her employment with the local newspaper and with the TV station. She also confirmed her friendship with Floyd.

With the facts known about her relationship with Floyd, the prosecutor requested that she be treated as a hostile witness. He insisted Daphne could be swayed in her answers by her personal feelings for the accused and by her obligations to the media.

I thought about objecting but couldn't understand how Daphne, being treated as hostile, could help the prosecution and remained silent. Floyd's testimony had obviously influenced the jury and I couldn't imagine anything Daphne could say that would cause them to doubt his testimony.

The prosecutor began by asking Daphne about the very first time she had seen Floyd, as he lay unconscious on the grass near his deceased grandmother. She repeated the testimony given previously by the Deputy Sheriff and her testimony led the jury nowhere. Then, to my surprise, the prosecutor began questioning Daphne about the tree. He questioned her in a way that made it obvious he was trying to discredit stories about the tree and to describe Floyd as being obsessed with the tree and the myths surrounding it.

He intimated that Floyd had used the wild stories as an excuse to place members of his family in dangerous situations. Daphne did her best to avoid being drawn into the warped picture the prosecutor was painting and as I listened to the new line of questioning, I realized he wasn't just trying to indict Floyd, he was also trying to trying to discredit the stories about the tree, and I had an idea why.

I knew about the Governor's campaign to stop all examinations of the tree and of his desire to have it destroyed, and was willing to bet the Governor had gotten to the prosecutor. The trial had suddenly become political and the prosecutor seemed to be making headway …. Until he asked Daphne the wrong question.

Daphne was under oath and to answer the prosecutor's question she was compelled to reveal the tree's secret. She hesitated but the prosecutor continued to push until she reluctantly explained the significance of the message in the tree.

"At first, I thought the stories Floyd told were myth," Daphne testified, "He told stories supposedly handed down from ancient Indian tribes and they were hard to believe. But teams of scientists have confirmed the tree is nearly fifty thousand years old, and just before coming here I was informed that they have discovered a mathematical message in its genetic code that had to have been placed there long before man became civilized. It is our first solid evidence of intelligent life before man and probably not of this planet."

Everyone in the courtroom was stunned and Floyd's indictment hearing was, for all practical purposes, over. The reporters at the rear and sides of the courtroom rushed for the exits anxious to file their stories, and no amount of gavel banging by the judge could restore order.

Having heard the relevant details surrounding Melissa Brenner's death and now the extraordinary news that the tree contained a message from another race of intelligent beings, the judge made a summery judgment against an indictment, and dismissed the jury. Floyd was free, but the tree had been indicted.

Unlike other news stories that diminish in importance as they spread from their source, Daphne's revelation spread around the planet as fast as it could be translated and transmitted. The Governor still wanted the tree cut down and continued to deny any message was in the trees DNA, but political expediency took precedence. If he destroyed the tree, he would be percieved by those who believed the message was real, as destroying the most important find in human history. The risk was too great and he quickly shifted his position, claiming Ohio was now the center of research into extraterrestrial life.

Most of those trying to find out more about the message in the tree consisted of the curious, but some of the protestors at the Brenner farm became more aggressive and set fires in the dry grass at the edges of the property. The press swarmed Dr. Brice's team forcing them to find relief by moving their staff and equipment to an undisclosed location. Other research teams gave up their investigations to avoid the confusion and returned to earlier projects. Public reactions and the demand for more information drove the press to extreme measures. Daphne found herself in the center of a media storm.

The message itself was of no help in explaining its purpose and, in a way, it was no message at all. Taken at its face value it was just an artifact of a long ago visit left wrapped in a microscopic biological package, waiting for a living form to evolve and read the code of life. The prime numbers probably meant nothing. They were most likely just a sign that couldn't be mistaken as an accident of nature, a pronouncement from one intelligent life form to another, like a message in a bottle set adrift, saying nothing except, *"We were here"*.

In spite of the initial excitement, life's normal routines continued. People around the world both welcomed and denounced the discovery, but only a few had enough surplus time to react or comment. Most people were too busy with everyday activities to give the finding much attention. They went to work, went shopping, boarded airplanes and met appointments. Except for a few scientists, hordes of reporters, and a few fanatics, human routines continued as usual.

Julia's Victorian home became a fortress surrounded by police doing their best to control a growing crowd of fanatics and reporters. Floyd, exhausted by the stress of the grand-jury hearings, sequestered himself inside and concentrated on preparing his paintings for their review by Julia's friend.

CHAPTER TWENTY-FIVE

Anxious to see Julia and review Floyd's paintings, Douglas closed his New York art gallery for the week, flew to Ohio, rented a car, and began his drive to Julia's house.

The Gallery in New York became Douglas's responsibility after his partner was killed in an accident. At first, it was a struggle to keep the gallery open. Before his partner's death he depended completely on his companion to run the gallery business and limited his contributions to providing his own paintings and scouting for new talent. After his partner's death, he struggled alone to balance the books and promote and show the works of new and promising artists. It had been difficult adjusting to the loss of his lover, but somehow he kept the supply of contemporary art moving and the cash flowing. It was only because of his persistence that the studio remained open.

An artist himself, Douglas was looking forward to seeing Floyd's paintings, especially since Julia recommended them. Julia had helped Douglas develop his own distinctive painting style, and if she saw promise in Floyd's work, he knew the trip would be worthwhile. During his flight to Ohio, Douglas remained insulated from the news of an alien message hidden in Floyd's tree, He was shocked when he turned on the rental car's radio and heard the news.

"The mysterious tree in Ohio took on an even greater significance today when a reporter testified in the trial of the tree's owner. Under oath, she disclosed that scientists examining the tree discovered an ancient message encoded in the tree's DNA. It is believed that an intelligent life form left the message thousands of years ago. Scientists working on the project in various countries have confirmed the findings and reactions to the news are mixed. The Catholic Church has refused comment until more is known, and the United States has declared the area around the tree to be a protected site until further tests can be conducted."

On hearing the news, Douglass realized he was no longer en-route to a relaxing reunion with an old friend and a review of a few paintings. Instead, he was zeroing in on an intergalactic event. The announcement on the radio added a large exclamation point to the words "promising artist", and as he drove up to Julia's house the exclamation point became even larger when he was stopped by the police.

"Sir this area is blocked off. You will have to go around."

The officer pointed down a side street leading away from Julia's house.

"I have an appointment with the owner of that house."

Douglas pointed at the large house directly in front of him.

"She is expecting me."

"I'm sorry." The police officer answered. "We can't allow anyone near the house, especially members of the press. You will have to go around!"

Frustrated, Douglas turned down the side street, parked his car and called Julia on his cell phone.

"Julia, I'm near your house but can't get through the police barricades. What's going on, are you being held hostage?"

"No, at least not by anyone inside, but the reporters outside are another story. Floyd is here and the reporters would be banging on the door if they weren't being kept away. Walk up to the corner and I will come out and get you."

Afraid she might be kept from returning to her own home, Julia got an officer's attention before she stepped off her porch. She explained that she was expecting the man who was walking toward them and he should be allowed to pass. She waited for Douglas on the sidewalk ignoring the shouting reporters as they tried to convince her that Floyd should step outside and make a statement. Julia had to shout to be heard above the din.

"Douglas, bring your suitcase with you. Once you're inside the wolf pack will never let you return to your car."

Julia pointed at the reporters being held back by police.

"You may as well plan on staying here tonight."

Douglas made his way past the crowd and. while Julia and Douglass exchanged greetings on the porch, Floyd, sat down at the piano and began to play. Inside the house art, music and preserved traditions from a more gentile time, held sway against the clamor outside, and Floyd felt safe.

Julia ushered Douglas inside, led him into the parlor and motioned for him to take a seat. Floyd continued to play, lost in his music, unaware of Douglas's presence. Floyd was still dressed in the suit and tie he had worn for court and his mask was in place. Floyd's attire and posture gave his recital a sense of formality befitting the classical piece he was playing.

Floyd played with his eyes closed and his head tipped back as if giving thanks for having been vindicated. He played with such emotion that an occasional tear ran down his cheek, and as Douglas listened, he was moved to the point of an occasional compulsive sob. Julia stood quietly behind Floyd with her hands folded over her heart.

Floyd's trial was over. His accusers had been silenced, but Floyd's tree was now accused of collaborating with aware beings from another time and another place. Humanity had once again lost its grip on the golden ring connecting it to the center of creation. The discomforting displacement caused by Aristarchus, Copernicus and Galileo was being felt again, but this time it was different. Five centuries of discovery had convinced most of humanity that we were not at the center of the universe, but now we were being told that, in addition to not occupying a center place in space, we were also not alone, and probably not the most advanced.

The cause of the new storm was not an astronomer but a young farmer and a tree. As the world struggled with the news, Floyd gave thanks for his redemption and celebrated inside his Victorian sanctuary with music.

When Floyd finished playing, Julia put her hands on his shoulders.

"Your music is as wonderful as your paintings and there is someone here to see them"

Forgetting he was wearing gloves, Floyd stood up and reached out to shake hands. Douglas glanced at Floyd's gloved hand and hesitated. Floyd immediately withdrew his greeting.

"I'm sorry, Floyd offered, "I sometimes forget about my gloves."

228

"I'm not offended." Douglas replied, "I didn't want to hurt you."

"My scars make a lot of things awkward but the pain is gone".

"Julia tells me you are a painter and have a gallery in New York."

Julia started for the kitchen.

"Since you two don't seem to need a formal introduction, I will get us something to drink. Why don't we stay in the parlor for a while and get acquainted. We can get to the paintings later."

Floyd was instantly at ease with his visitor. Douglas had a gentle demeanor that Floyd found attractive and Douglas seemed genuinely interested in how Floyd was coping with his ordeal.

CHAPTER TWENTY-SIX

After taping her news report of the trial, Daphne left the TV station intending to go directly home, but discovered reporters waiting outside her apartment. To avoid the media pack she drove to Julia's house but found her house surrounded by press and police as well. As a last resort, she came to my house and when she reached my driveway, she stayed in her car and called to check on Floyd.

"Julia, I need to speak to Floyd but he isn't answering his phone. Is he with you?"

"Yes he is here. If you want to come to the house I will have to get you past the police."

"I'm at his lawyer's house now. Can I stop by in a few minuets?"

"Of course," Julia answered, "Douglas from New York is here to review Floyd's paintings and I'm certain Floyd would want you here to see what Douglas thinks."

Daphne finished her call and knocked on my door.

"I was on my way home," Daphne explained, "but there were a bunch of reporters waiting so I went to Julia's. Her house was also under siege so I came here."

"Why aren't they bothering you?"

"I suppose they think I don't know anything about the message in the tree, and they're right, or maybe they just don't want to deal with a lawyer."

We were both worried about Floyd being able to decompress after the trial, but there were additional reasons we needed to see him. Daphne's reasons were emotional mine were legal.

Unwilling to leave my daughter at home, I insisted she come too. I expected Jenny to object but instead she welcomed the opportunity to visit her favorite storyteller and avoid her homework.

When we arrived at Julia's the same officer that forced Douglas to park on a side street tried to divert us. Julia was quick to tell the officer to let us through and we parked in her driveway.

Once inside we joined Floyd and Douglas in the parlor. Julia offered us refreshments and after introductions, we joined the ongoing conversation. Floyd was describing his obsession to paint only one thing, the tree, and Douglas was explaining how many of the young painters, whose works he displayed, had similar compulsions. The strong rapport between the two men was obvious, and it made Daphne nervous.

Julia interrupted. "Why don't we continue this in my studio so Douglas can see some of Floyd's paintings?"

We followed the two painters down the long hallway where paintings hung on both walls. A few were Julia's, but most were paintings done by her many students. Douglas stopped in front of a painting he recognized.

"I'm honored." Douglas said, pointing at a small painting. "This was one of my earliest works, and if I remember correctly, you had a lot of criticism."

"Yes I did," Julia replied. "And if I had been truthful about your raw talent instead of pointing out ways in which you could improve, you would still be painting like that. You tell me if you are now a better painter and also tell me if your ego is now a bit more in check."

Douglas laughed and asked Floyd if Julia was as rough on him.

"I think she feels sorry for me," Floyd answered, "and I don't want anyone to do that. I have no idea if my paintings are good, or even why I paint them. I see what I want to put on the canvas before I begin and then I use the brushes and mix the paints the way Julia taught me. After that, it all seems natural."

We entered the studio to find Floyds paintings neatly displayed on easels and shelves. Julia had arranged them for Douglas to review and had removed or turned over other paintings to avoid any distractions. Light from the skylights was fading as Douglas went slowly from one painting to another. He picked each one up and carried it to the brightest spot in the room. He didn't speak, and his face remained expressionless. Floyd was nervous but didn't want to interfere with the evaluation. He moved to a corner of the room, away from Douglas's examinations.

He seemed embarrassed by the attention his paintings were being given.

Daphne instinctively moved close to Floyd. She still felt the same rush of emotion whenever she was near him but was afraid she might have been too bold, and maybe even blind. She had committed herself, even given herself to Floyd but now, she was beginning to sense he might not feel the same way.

As everyone waited for Douglas to complete his evaluation Floyd asked Daphne about her testimony in court.

"You said in court there was a message from the past hidden in the tree that couldn't have been put there by humans. What message, what did it say?"

"The message was a number sequence. Do you know what a prime number is?"

"I have heard of them," Floyd answered, "but I don't know exactly what they are. Is the message important?"

"Yes. The scientists found an unusual sequence of markers in the tree's DNA. At first, they thought it was just an accident but the sequence was repeated. Eventually they figured out the sequences were prime numbers and couldn't be an accident. They also discovered that the markers were inserted many thousands of years ago, long before mankind knew anything about prime numbers, or DNA."

"Are they sure?" Floyd asked.

"Yes they seem quite sure."

Floyd thought about what Daphne had just told him for a moment and then turned to the rest of us.

"If I'm going to continue to paint the tree," he announced, "I may have to paint-by-number.

It took a while for Floyd's dry humor to sink in. Jenny was the first to laugh. She had just finished a paint-by-number project and instantly associated it with the numbers in the tree's DNA.

I was the last to appreciate Floyd's humor and Jenny became exasperated trying to explain it to me. After everyone stopped laughing at the joke and at my naïveté, I realized that my worries about Floyd being depressed were probably unwarranted.

Douglas finished his examination of the paintings and held one up as an example.

"These are exquisite works of art." He began. "I expected something rough with heavy strong brush strokes but these are refined, deliberate, and full of emotion. They all have the same twisted tree as their subject but each is unique with its own perspective. Individually and as a collection the paintings are exceptionally well suited for showing and I would be honored to have them in my gallery."

"That's wonderful." Julia clapped her hands. "The tree and Floyd are already famous and the paintings should demand a good price. What do you think they will sell for?"

"As a collector's item they should bring a few thousand each, but these are truly works of art and they need to be appreciated before we put a price tag on them. I would like to show them without an offering first, and then take them to auction, if Floyd agrees."

Floyd got up off the bench he and Daphne were sharing and walked away from her. He shook Douglas's hand and hugged him. He then turned to Julia.

"You are my angel." Floyd said. "You gave me a safe place full of ideas and opportunities, I thought the tree might have been cursed and the curse might have spread to me, but now everything has turned around, thank you."

Douglas put his arm around Floyd and the two of them walked out of the studio with the rest of us following. Daphne was the last through the door, and as she watched, Douglas and Floyd walk arm in arm she knew she had made a mistake. Floyd could never love her and she would probably never stop loving him.

When we reached the parlor, Daphne sat next to me, away from Floyd. I sensed her discomfort and asked if she was ok. She gave me a half smile but didn't answer.

After a round of congratulations, the conversation turned to the meaning of the message in the tree. Jenny brought the subject up by telling Floyd she thought his joke about painting by number was cool, and that she really liked the stories he told about the tree at his pig roasts. She thought his stories were better than a tree full of numbers.

I had to agree. The stories he told were at least believable, the story Dr. Brice was telling made no sense. Why would anyone place coded numbers into a plant and what purpose could hidden mathematics serve? I agreed that Floyd's stories were more plausible.

Douglas had been in route to Julia's when the news of Dr. Brice's findings unfolded and he didn't have all the details, but he did have an opinion.

"What if the message wasn't meant for us? "Or, what if it isn't a message at all?"

Douglas was alluding to our egocentric tendency to assume that everything was created for humans. Even with direct evidence that another intelligent life form existed, we didn't want to accept it, but if they were real and had indeed left a message, we assumed it had to be meant for us. It would take more than a message from an alien to prove that man was not the center of all existence.

Jenny jumped back into the conversation.

"Maybe they were just leaving their mark, like carving their initials onto a tree or a dog peeing on a fire hydrant."

Julia laughed.

"Pretty elaborate graffiti, and what is a prime number anyway?"

CHAPTER TWENTY-SEVEN

After a week of intense public interest, news coverage of the tree's numerical message began to fade and most of the world's population refocused their attention on more entertaining events, like the next Hollywood movie or the next soccer match. Not even a note from an alien intelligence could trump the latest action thriller.

If aliens wanted to get humanity's attention, they would need a much bigger event, or an easier to understand message. Cerebral aliens were not very interesting, but the tree itself and the giant dome covering it remained newsworthy, and continued to generate myths.

After arranging for the safe shipment of Floyd's paintings Douglas returned to New York and began preparing for the showing. Floyd remained safe in his apartment and took advantage of Julia's extensive library to learn more about the message left in his tree especially number theory and the relationship of prime numbers to composite numbers.

Floyd and Douglas spoke on the phone nearly every day and exchanged regular e-mails discussing the details of Floyd's upcoming debut as an artist. Daphne called Floyd occasionally but didn't visit. She had misinterpreted his "lost puppy" affections for love and she regretted her advances.

She recognized Floyd's suppressed sexuality, and was reconciled to the fact that his affections could never be directed toward her, or any other woman.

Daphne continued her contact with Dr. Brice and he reminded her of her promise to acquire Floyd's medical records. With the disclosure, that the tree might be a point of contact with other intelligent beings, its protection seemed assured, however, one could never be certain, and Dr. Brice wanted to continue his scientific inquiries.

Floyd had previously agreed to cooperate but would have to sign a release and provide blood and skin samples. Daphne made the arrangements, set a date, and, to avoid the press, arrived at Julia's house early in the morning to take Floyd to the hospital.

When they arrived at the hospital, Dr. Brice was waiting in the hospital's lobby. He had already talked to Floyd's doctor about the extent of Floyd's burns and had gotten the doctor's opinion about the peculiar nature of the sticky substance that caused them. He explained his reasons for having Floyd's blood drawn and his scars reexamined and asked for cheek swabs to check for any DNA abnormalities.

The procedure took only a few minuets but Dr. Brice wanted more information from Floyd about his contact with the tree, and Floyd wanted to know what Dr. Brice was looking for in his DNA. Daphne also had unanswered questions and wanted to be brought up to speed on any new scientific findings regarding the tree. Daphne suggested the three of them go to the hospital cafeteria for coffee.

Daphne was still carrying the promissory spoon in her purse and remembering her first experience with the cafeteria's dirty silverware, opted to drink her coffee black. She still felt an obligation to Floyd even though he had been exonerated of any complicity in his grandmother's death. But his life was still being disrupted by questions surrounding the tree, and his ownership of the farm remained in doubt if the government exercised imminent domain.

The medical findings would play an important part in determining Floyd's future, and Daphne wanted to know what Dr. Brice was planning. No reporters had followed them but to be safe, they found a corner table away from others in the cafeteria.

Floyd asked his first question before they were seated.

"What are you looking for in these tests, and what are you going to do with the results?"

"I was originally looking for a reason for the CDC to quarantine the farm to prevent the governor from having the tree destroyed. Now, with the news of the tree's strange DNA the Fed's are involved, and many people will be asking for samples from both the tree and you. Truthfully, I wish we were wrong about the prime number thing but I can't come up with any other explanation. The markers had to be implanted when the tree was in an embryonic state and the trees age has been confirmed in several different ways. As far as I can tell it cannot be an accident, it cannot be a fake, and humans couldn't have done it. There is a lot of junk DNA in all genomes. Only about ten percent translates into the proteins that make up any living physical form. The rest seems to be left over from earlier experiments by nature and the tree has a lot of junk DNA.

We were lucky to have spotted the markers. They show up as little dashes on a print out and are mixed with lots of other little dashes. If one of my grad students hadn't taken a copy home and if her math major roommate hadn't been curious and counted the dashes, we would never have found the sequence."

Daphne wasn't satisfied with Dr. Brice's answer.

"If you don't need quarantine anymore, why do you need Floyd's blood and DNA? What are you really looking for?"

Dr. Brice sipped his coffee and hesitated before answering.

"If Floyd had been stung by an unknown insect or bitten by an animal we would be worried about an infection or an allergic reaction. Floyd had some of his flesh dissolved by a substance secreted by a living thing we can't categorize. We want to know more about the tree but we also need to know more about it's defenses and if there are any lasting effects from contact. Floyd is the only person that we know of that has been in contact with the tree's sap."

"Not so." Daphne answered. "Floyd's Minister was also burned. He was burned on his hand while he was trying to help Floyd cope with his father's death."

"Is that right?" Dr. Brice sat up straight. "Can we get in touch with this person? A second sample would be invaluable."

"I can put you in touch," Daphne answered, "but you have to keep Floyd and me in the loop, whatever your findings."

"I'll do my best, but these tests are out of my field. Geneticists and other specialists will be examining the samples and drawing their own conclusions. I hope to set up an oversight committee to coordinate the investigations and collect the results, but it may be out of my hands. The best I can hope for is to retain access to the tree, and access to some of the DNA results."

Daphne instinctively took the spoon out of her purse and began tapping it on the table.

"The scientific implications are important but so is Floyd. This could easily turn into a witch-hunt with Floyd becoming a warlock. Can you guarantee that won't happen?"

Daphne's feelings for Floyd were still prompting her to behave like a mother protecting a child. Part of it was empathy for a naïve soul thrown into untenable situations and part of it was her continuing romantic feelings. Being in love with someone who could never return her love was maddening, but she still wouldn't let anyone hurt him. When Daphne finally stopped talking, she noticed she was tapping the spoon and put it away, suggested they adjourn their meeting, drove Floyd back to Julia's house, and drove directly to my office.

I was starting to prepare Floyd's claim against the government to maintain control of his property, but I wasn't having much success. I couldn't find many precedents and welcomed Daphne's interruption.

"I'm glad you're here Daphne, would you like some coffee?"

Daphne shook her head and held up the spoon.

"I need to be done with this. I've gotten much too involved and need to move on. I just came from the hospital where they collected blood and DNA samples from Floyd as if he was a guinea pig. Dr. Brice and many others will soon be sorting through Floyd's biological makeup like detectives. I am an interested party and a friend, but I am also a part of the media and supposedly, a journalist. I can't do my job if I am at the center of the story. Floyd has a place to hide, a new career, and lots of support. I'm alone and feel like I'm trapped in something I didn't choose and can't control."

Daphne slid the spoon across the table to me, put her head down and began to sob. I laid the spoon aside, went around the table, put my hand on her shoulder and tried to comfort her.

"You're right. You were drawn into this by accident, and by me. If I hadn't made you promise to help me when we first met, you would be busy working other stories. But who knows how it would have turned out if you hadn't been there. We can't go back, but you don't have to go on. Floyd is trapped by events he can't control and they will continue to follow him. You've done all you can. It's ok to stop. Forget the damn spoon. It's ok to stop."

I lifted my hand from Daphne's shoulder, walked back to the spoon and tossed it into the wastebasket. Daphne stopped sobbing, sat up, and dried her eyes.

"I'm sorry," She said. "I shouldn't have come here."

"No, you came to the right place. I understand your dilemma. You developed strong feelings for Floyd but there isn't anything more you can do. It's time to get on with your life and your career. Why don't you take a short vacation?"

Daphne was quiet. She got up and walked to the door.

"Your right," She answered. "I can't help anymore and I need to get away from this and away from my job. A vacation is a good idea."

I responded without thinking. "Why not come with Jenny and me to New York. We always take a vacation this time of the year and were planning to see Floyd's exhibition and then tour the Big Apple. Jenny likes you, and I would love to have you join us. Extra supervision for my much-to energetic and imaginative daughter would help me and it might help you clean the slate if you could see Floyd beginning a new life as an artist."

Daphne didn't give me a definite answer but promised to think about it. I presented the vacation idea to Jenny over dinner and she was enthusiastic, maybe a bit too enthusiastic. I was very strict with Jenny and suspected she liked the idea of Daphne coming with us, not because she liked Daphne, but because she thought she might get away with a few more things if my attention was diverted.

Daphne put Dr. Brice in contact with Floyd's minister and arranged for a few weeks away from her journalistic responsibilities. With the spoon in the wastebasket, Daphne's mood improved rapidly and she decided to accompany Jenny and me to New York.

To help prepare for our trip she searched for hotels and Broadway events we might enjoy and called upon a journalist friend in New York to help arrange tickets. She also took Jenny to lunch and involved her in the planning. With Jenny and Daphne busy planning and shopping, I caught up on my work and had a chance to follow up on the latest findings regarding the tree.

Very little new information was available. Dr Brice continued to maintain that the tree remained unidentified because matching the trees DNA to other plants was a slow process, and with almost one thousand tree species in the United States and with nearly ten thousand more throughout the world, finding a good match was difficult. Getting cooperation with testing labs in other countries was also difficult, and the government had reassigned responsibility for protecting the tree to Homeland Security and responsibility for testing to the National Institute of Health. I learned that Dr. Brice had convinced Floyd's minister to give samples of his DNA for testing only after assuring him they were looking for disease and not a demonic possession.

The minister's background and education left him naïve as to modern science or medicine but he couldn't avoid the information that surrounded him. What he found essential and useful he incorporated into his lexicon, the rest he buried and replaced with more understandable and less threatening explanations.

He accepted DNA as a reality but denied evolution and the image of the number seven burned into his hand drove him to find religious assurances that supernatural forces hadn't taken over his soul.

Because of the minister's paranoia, and because Dr. Brice wanted a second lab to evaluate the blood and DNA of another burn victim, he sent the minister to an outside clinic for a complete work up. The Clinic took the same samples taken from Floyd but with the addition of semen samples. The minister took the request for reproductive samples as clear evidence that his DNA had been contaminated. He left the Clinic convinced that he was carrying the seeds of aliens.

CHAPTER TWENTY-EIGHT

Jenny completed her fifth grade school year and after a lazy week, Daphne, Jenny and I were on our way to New York.

At first, the trip was full of excitement, but as the miles rolled on Jenny became bored and Daphne started a songfest. It kept Jenny busy but drove me crazy. We reached our hotel just before I had a nervous breakdown and while Daphne and Jenny cleaned up for dinner, I went to the bar for a much-needed martini.

At the bar, I check on missed phone calls. My messages were all work related except for one. Dr. Brice had left a message that Floyd's minister was upset about having his DNA tested and had disappeared. The news worried me but I decided to keep it to myself. I had enough to worry about with Daphne's depresion and Jenny's exuberance, and put my phone and work matters on hold.

My concern about Jenny taking advantage of Daphne's presence proved groundless. Her new chaperone was just as strict as I had ever been, and in spite of her short leash, Jenny seemed to be enjoying the trip. When Jenny was given a choice of roommates, she asked if Daphne snored, and immediately agreed to stay with Daphne in an adjoining room. Without Jenny waking me every few hours to tell me to be quiet, I too got a good night's sleep.

The next morning, after lengthy primping delays by the girls and a late breakfast, we took a taxi to Douglas's Gallery for the debut of Floyd's artwork. The Gallery was located between an upscale restaurant and a jewelry store not far from Times Square. We arrived a few minutes before the Gallery doors opened and while we waited, Daphne and Jenny amused each other by pretending to be rich and picked out the most expensive things on the menu displayed in the window of the restaurant and the most expensive pieces of jewelry displayed in the jewelry store's window. While the girls played their game, a small crowd began to gather on the sidewalk in front of the

Gallery. At first, I thought the crowd was waiting to see Floyd's artwork, but then I noticed the signs. The signs were kept covered and I couldn't read them. I assumed they were protest slogans and their presence made me nervous. By the time the Gallery was scheduled to open, there were almost a dozen sign holders on the sidewalk. When the doors actually opened, we skirted the crowd and entered quickly.

The Gallery lobby was small but well appointed. It had marble floors, an ornate ceiling and frescos covered the walls. Two marble statues guarded the entrance to the gallery in the back of the lobby. On one side, a formally dressed attendant was pouring coffee and offering canapés. We presented our tickets and were immediately greeted by Douglas. He welcomed us and then began exchanging greetings with others as they found their way through the growing crowd outside.

"Who are the people on the sidewalk?" asked one of the visitors.

Douglas was unaware of the crowd and stuck his head out the door to see what was happening. The few individuals we had seen had now grown to a crowd of over twenty, most of them with signs. They were obviously here to protest the tree, and or Floyd. Douglas reentered the lobby somewhat alarmed but with a smile on his face.

"I have to make a quick phone call." He announced. "I will be right back and introduce you to a collection that has become famous even before being exhibited. Please take advantage of the canapés and coffee."

When Douglas returned, he told us he had made two phone calls, the first to a local TV station to let them know about the gathering protest and a second to the police.

"I don't want trouble," he explained, "but the protest is obviously about the tree, so why not turn their protest into free advertising? It will bring additional art critics and hundreds of curious visitors to the Gallery to see Floyd's paintings."

TV cameras arrived first, followed almost immediately by several police cars. A spokesperson for the group welcomed the cameras and explained their opposition to any promotion of the "Tree of Evil". The group demanded that all paintings of the tree be destroyed.

The small protest would have gone unnoticed and probably never broadcast, but for the arrival of the police.

The protesters were quickly disbursed for not having a permit, but not before their protest had been turned into an unintentional promotion of Floyd's paintings.

Inside, Douglas led us into the heart of the Gallery. Floyd's paintings were professionally displayed on the gallery walls and around each painting were large prime numbers. The contrast between Floyd's emotional paintings and the emotionless numbers was striking.

The numbers around the first few paintings ranged from single digits to five digits and the numbers grew progressively longer as one went around the room. On the first wall, the numbers were single and double-digit prime numbers. On the last wall, very long twenty digit prime numbers stretched around and behind the paintings. A small plaque near the entrance to the gallery gave a short explanation of the trees significance, and a similar plaque at the exit introduced the artist and announced a future auction.

I was impressed by both the display and by the paintings.

"If the aliens that marked the tree could see this, I bet they would also be impressed." I commented

"I asked Jenny what she thought.

"Wow," Jenny said as she took it all in, "they look different in here, really special. I like it."

"Me too," responded Daphne, "presented like this they are very special, very professional, and the way they are arranged you can see Floyd's transition from being dominated by the tree to controlling it."

Daphne had noticed that the paintings were arranged chronologically and one could see the progression of Floyd's emotional perception of the tree change from his first paintings to the last. A progression of style was also evident as Floyd's skill with the brush improved, but the greatest change was hidden from those in the gallery who didn't know the artist. The greatest change was in the artist himself.

We all stood back to appreciate the arrangement and to marvel at the large number of paintings. Floyd had been very prolific.

Eventually we found Floyd in the crowd and congratulated him. He was dressed in a casual suit with a more stylish mask in place. His beard was trimmed short and he spoke with a newfound assurance enabled by an expanded vocabulary acquired from Julia's library. The naïve unsophisticated farmer had emerged from his emotional cocoon a debonair celebrity, confidently discussing art with aficionados. Even his stature and mannerisms had changed. Bent by years of heavy lifting, the slight slouch that marked him as a tradesman had been replaced by an erect posture more typical of the social élite.

Douglas was probably responsible for Floyd's new image and before we could ask about his striking transition, Douglas approached, put a protective hand on Floyd's shoulder and turned to Daphne.

"What do you think of the presentation?" Douglas asked.

"It is marvelous." Daphne answered. "And your presentation of the artist himself is also very impressive."

Douglas smiled and gave Floyd a friendly pat.

"It took some convincing," Douglas bragged, "but he finally agreed to a complete makeover by a friend of mine, and after one look, we knew we had a new Floyd, someone just as impressive as his paintings."

Daphne turned toward Floyd.

"I'm happy for you," Daphne said, "Your new life looks good on you and I'm certain you will be successful."

I could tell from Daphne's tone that she preferred the old, less pretentious Floyd, but she knew the Floyd she had cared for was gone. Daphne put her arm through mine and drew Jenny close to her as a signal to Floyd that she too was moving on. I knew the gesture wasn't meant for me, but I couldn't help but feel, for a moment, that I had a complete family again.

As the crowd in the studio grew, we mingled with the onlookers and listened to their comments. Most of the gallery visitors were aware of the significance of the tree and of the artist's struggles, and were full of praise. Their compliments, genuine or not, would publicize the upcoming auction, and combined with the media coverage of the protestors outside, would drive up the bidding.

Daphne felt better after meeting the new Floyd. It allowed her to let go of her misplaced attachment to the Floyd she had met in the hospital. The old Floyd was gone, transformed, and soon to be even more famous than the tree.

CHAPTER TWENTY-NINE

After our experience at the gallery, I indulged my female companions by taking them to lunch at the restaurant where they had pretended to order the most expensive items from the menu in the window.

Jenny stayed on course and ordered an expensive quiche. Daphne was more reasonable in her selection and didn't appear to be hungry. Her mood, however, was much improved and she jokingly handed me a spoon from the table and told me to put it in my pocket. Jenny hadn't been privy to the significance of the promissory spoon, and reacted.

"Are you crazy?" The waiter is looking right at you. If you're going to steal silverware, do it when nobody is looking!"

Daphne and I laughed and assured Jenny that we weren't really serious, and for the first time since our Floydian adventures had begun, it was true, we weren't being serious, neither of us needed to protect Floyd any longer.

After lunch, we visited Time Square and returned to the hotel to get ready to attend a Broadway show. Daphne was excellent with Jenny and didn't mind sharing her room. She helped Jenny with her hair and gave Jenny her first experience with makeup. I was stunned at how pretty my little girl really was and saddened that she was growing up.

We enjoyed the Broadway presentation but Daphne was not feeling well and I decided to cut our New York vacation short. The next morning, on our way out of the hotel, Daphne picked up a newspaper and before we got to the car, she scanned the front page.

"Oh my God!" she exclaimed. "Just when we thought it was over, it starts again."

I took the paper from her and read the headlines aloud.

"Preacher Sells Sperm After Contact With DNA From Alien Tree."

Daphne was angry.

"First this guy preaches love and forgiveness, then he convinces himself the tree is evil, and now this. Why do people listen to these quacks'?"

"Is it possible that his DNA could carry something from the tree?" I asked.

"He was burned, like Floyd, but it was superficial." Daphne answered. "He had genetic tests but I seriously doubt that DNA can transfer by contact with skin and it is highly unlikely that it could alter his sperm. Start driving while I call Dr. Brice."

Dr. Brice had seen the headlines and was as shocked as Daphne that a minister of the gospel would resort to such a misguided act. Dr. Brice had arranged the testing of the minister's DNA only to be certain he wasn't carrying any pathogens. The lab had gone further than he requested and tested not only the minister's blood but also his sperm. Dr Brice doubted that tree sap could transfer DNA, especially to reproductive cells, but he wasn't made privy to the test results. He promised to contact the lab and to get back to us as soon as possible.

Daphne turned toward me as she turned off her cell phone.

"I wonder if Floyd has seen the news this morning."

"It's not our problem any more," I answered. "The spoon is in the waste basket. Does anyone know where the minister went?"

Jenny joined the conversation from the back seat.

"What is it with you two and spoons? I don't get it."

"It's not really about spoons," I answered. "It's about promises, I'll explain later"

The drive home was quiet. The excitement of the trip to New York was gone. The few moments of freedom from the infectious myths surrounding the tree were gone, but the myths had reappeared, and once again, we were trapped.

Daphne would certainly be asked to follow the story of a preacher trying to make money by propagating an alien race, and I was certain to be drawn into the new tangle of events as Floyd's lawyer of record. I began to wish I had never gone to Floyd's pig roasts.

Having overheard me read the headlines aloud in New York, my ten year old had a question.

"What's sperm?" Jenny asked from the back seat.

Daphne gave me a look with eyebrows raised that said, "Ok dad, answer that one!"

For a moment, I was stumped.

Daphne just grinned and Jenny leaned forward from the back seat, also grinning. I could see her expression in the car's rear view mirror and realized that my innocent little Jenny was setting me up. I was embarrassed and angry at the same time but I had to answer, so I skirted the subject.

"According to Aristotle, sperm is purified blood. That's why we talk of being related by blood."

Daphne clapped her hands and laughed. Jenny leaned back with a disappointed look on her face and remained quiet for the rest of the trip.

We were almost home when Dr. Brice called back.

"I talked to the testing lab and citing HIPPA laws, they refused to disclose their findings. I tried to explain that the minister had indirectly disclosed the results but they still wouldn't grant my request for fear of legal repercussions."

"My suggestion," Dr Brice continued, "is to see if Floyd will release his records and see if there is any truth to the minister's claim that might have driven him to such a rash act. If the tree is able to alter human reproductive DNA, we may have a real problem with the minister spreading alien seed all over the place.

We arrived home after dark and I dropped Daphne off at her apartment. The next morning I dropped Jenny at one of her friends and went to my office. There was still the issue of Floyd's property rights to his farm, and now, with his minister putting his DNA into question, Floyd could be suspected of harboring the genesis of an alien race. His preference in sexual partners would make the point moot but Floyd had no control over public perceptions and perceptions were again taking precedence over facts.

The news concerning the minister's activities escalated when the CDC, fearing a health hazard, tried to track him down and attempted to confiscate sperm he had sold to fertility clinics and reproductive centers. The minister was being paid exorbitant fees for his, *supposed alien DNA* and the samples were being divided into smaller packets and resold for even higher dollar amounts. Tracing all of the samples became impossible, and a black market for alien seed developed.

There was no proof that the tree had affected his DNA, and doubt remained that the prime number message was real. The species and exact age of the tree were still unknown and myths continued to grow.

The intense scientific interest in the tree was giving wild theories credibility, and before a standard of proof could be established or proper investigations conducted, people were beginning to believe whatever they were told. Unproven theories and mythical synergy became a cult ideology and the press continued to milk it for ratings.

Several new religions sprang up and developed cult followings. A religious backlash developed nearly as quickly and ministers, priests and imams spoke from podiums and pulpits to hundreds of millions of the faithful in an attempt to explain away the feverish acclaim given the new advent of a mysterious visitation.

Unfortunately, the more the establishment tried to debunk the myths the more attention they received. Even negative press added interest and converts. With alien seed available, and woman willing to host a new race, thousands volunteered to bear hybrid children. The Church of the New World and The Church of The Double Helix soon became established denominations. Money poured in to create birthing centers and provide prenatal care for the mother's of the new race.

The new myths contained just enough scientific information to engage and energize the secular, and just enough religious mysticism to attract any faltering faithful. The number of potential converts was enormous and cults grew rapidly.

The minister's naïveté and greed had sparked the "sacred seed" religions and resurrected the oldest and most basic of human conflicts, a conflict of perspectives. The minister was at the center of the conflict and those who believed the seed was now encoded in human DNA either worshiped the minister as the chosen vessel for a new world order, or as a mutant threat from an alien invader.

The wave of hysteria created by the minister's actions drew Floyd out of the comfort of his newfound fame and back into a world filled with accusations. The new myths were becoming dangerous for Floyd and potentially dangerous for Daphne. Out of fear, she came to me for advice.

CHAPTER THIRTY

Daphne arrived at my office unannounced.

"I'm pregnant," She blurted out. "And Floyd is the father."

I was stunned. I was aware of the new myths related to the tree and the turmoil they were creating, but finding Daphne with child was a shock.

Floyd had already called me for advice on how to protect himself from the hysteria and now Daphne was leaning on me as well. I liked them both but felt helpless and had my doubts than any of it was true.

"Does Floyd know you are pregnant?" I asked.

"No," Daphne answered, "I wasn't certain until this morning, and I don't know how to tell him. This will probably destroy him and it may destroy me. What do I do?"

"First, sit down so we can talk and try to figure this out. Can I have my secretary get you coffee or a sweet roll?"

Daphne gagged and shook her head, 'No'.

"I'm sorry," I said, "I wasn't thinking. When did you first suspect you might be pregnant?"

"The Idea began to frighten me when Floyd's minister went crazy and started selling his sperm. I began having morning sickness while we were in New York."

"This is confidential, isn't it? I mean privileged client attorney information?"

"As far as I'm concerned it's confidential but unless you retain me as your legal council it isn't privileged. If you want our conversation to be privileged put a dollar on the table and I'll have my secretary draw up a retainer."

Daphne reached into her purse and handed me a dollar.

"God I hope this doesn't turn out like the spoon."

It took awhile to calm Daphne, but when she finally relaxed, she became rational and helped me lay out her options. Her first decision was to keep her pregnancy secret until she could make sense out of her choices. Her second decision was to seek the facts regarding human DNA being affected by the tree's sap. The rush to sell and spread the minister's sperm had gotten ahead of any real findings. The investigation into both the minister's and Floyd's DNA was ongoing and had reached no definite conclusions.

"As long as my pregnancy remains secret, I am protected from public hysteria," Daphne offered, "but if the press gets hold of it, I become either the mother of Satan or the mother of a divine intervention. Either way my child, if it's allowed to live, will have no chance for a normal life.

Daphne was desperate.

"What if we could find a doctor that could test the DNA of my baby and keep a secret?"

"I'm not certain that will help, and I'm not sure it's safe. If it's taking this long for teams of geneticists to sort through the DNA of the minister you may be changing diapers before you get an answer. I think you are going to have to decide without proof."

"You mean guess."

"No, I mean take what you know and use your instinct. We like to think we always need facts to make a wise choice but even facts change over time. We aren't even certain the prime number sequence they found in the tree is really an insert. Maybe it is just an attribute of nature like a Fibonacci spiral. You can't depend on doctors, scientists, or anyone else to decide if the replicating DNA inside you has been altered. Hell, every child's DNA is altered. It is changed by being a random mix of the DNA of its parents and by random faults and errors that are inevitable in any sentence that contains several million letters. The best answer we are ever going to get will come from inside your head. You have to decide if the stories are true or if they are myth, and until you decide, you will be at the mercy of the tree."

"Damn you," Daphne responded. I came to you for help and you dump my problem right back in my lap."

"Please don't think of it that way. I want to help but we need a starting point. If we assume you are carrying an intentionally altered being we have to decide if that is a good thing or a bad thing, and all the decisions that follow come from our first assumption. If we assume you are carrying a normal child, we have a very different set of choices to make. We can't follow both paths."

"And how can I possibly know I'm making the right choice?" Daphne asked with tears in he eyes.

I was desperate, just as desperate as Daphne, and without thinking, the words just poured out of my mouth. I surprised myself by suggesting prayer. I was definitely not religious and thought of prayer as a submissive mental state taught by priests for control purposes, and yet here I was, suggesting that Daphne pray.

"You once told me you weren't religious but had an experience that made you think prayers might be answered. If it worked once, why not try it again?"

"You're right." Daphne answered. "I have to decide and I would like to pray. I prayed before in the hospital chapel. Can you take me there?"

I took Daphne to the hospital and waited while she sought an answer. She was quiet when she came out and

I knew better than to ask her about her experience. As we got into the car, she handed me a pamphlet.

"I want to go here."

I read the pamphlet and was shocked. The pamphlet was titled: "The Right to Choose". It was a brochure from an abortion clinic not far from the hospital.

"I thought you were going to the chapel."

"I did. This was on the seat when I started to sit down. I took it as a sign. The clinic offers counseling by a physician and I need someone who can listen to me with an open mind and a doctor that deals with birth decisions every day seems like a good place to start."

My first impulse was to try to talk her out of entertaining the idea of having an abortion, but it wasn't my place to question her decision, and finding an abortion pamphlet waiting on a chair in a chapel was almost miraculous. I suggested she call the number on the pamphlet before we walked in unannounced.

CHAPTER THIRTY-ONE

The errant minister was also desperate. He had created a monster that threatened to destroy him and he felt safe only when he was moving. He moved from city to city contacting quasi-legitimate reproductive centers, collecting thousands of dollars for each sample and then moved on.

Groups of religious extremists, who wanted him stopped, were tracking him, as were members of new cults who wanted to give him sanctuary. The FBI was also seeking him for interstate fraud. He trusted no one. If he surrendered to the FBI or sought sanctuary with the leaders of the cults, his lucrative income would end and greed continued to drive him. If religious extremists caught up with him the consequences could be fatal, but he believed he was doing the work of God. Why else would so many be willing to pay for his seed?

The minister had been traveling in circles around the US and had just revisited a clinic in Ohio when he noticed a small group of men following him. To avoid them he took a shortcut to the parking garage trying to get to his car. He made it as far as the garage elevator where four men surrounded him. He knew he couldn't outrun them and had no choice but to enter the elevator. The men said nothing as they got onto the elevator behind him. He was trapped and as soon as the elevator doors closed, he knew he was being abducted. One of the men pushed the emergency stop button and with the elevator stopped between floors the men blind folded and gagged him. With his hands tied behind his back, the minister was dragged from the elevator, shoved into a van, and driven to a cemetery where his blindfold and gag were removed.

It was almost dark but the minister could see a church at the edge of the graveyard and began to plead with his abductors.

"Look," the minister pleaded, "I'm not hurting anyone. This was meant to be and I just doing God's work. If you want money I can arrange for it, but you don't need to do this, I'm an innocent victim"

"The abductors remained silent and when the minister began to scream, replaced his gag and ignored his muffled cries. The tallest of the men brought a pair of hedge clippers from their van. He held it in front of the minister's face and clicked the blades. The minister had expected to be killed, this was worse.

"My God, No," he pleaded through his gag, "please No!"

The men had no compassion. The tall one answered with impunity.

"You're spreading an evil seed. You and every vial of seed, and every woman pregnant with your seed and every child born of the seed, has to be destroyed."

Two of the men pulled the minister's pants off and held him while the man with the clippers castrated him.

The minister tried to scream through his gag, but no one came to help. The men left him bleeding and semiconscious propped up against a tombstone. The evening chill and the cold headstone brought kept him partial conscious. The men had removed his blindfold and made him watch while they mutilate him but his gag was still in place and he couldn't call for help. He remembered the church and with his pants dragging behind began to crawl toward the lights shining through the church's stained glass windows. With his hands still tied, he inched along like a worm. The pain was excruciating and he was week from loss of blood, but eventually he reached the church and began to crawl along its foundation wall. He wanted to reach the front of the building, instead he came to a large uncovered window-well and as he tried to crawl around it, his dragging pants caught on a corner and he tumbled in.

The window well was too deep for him to crawl out and in his delirium; he thought he had fallen into an open grave. Fortunately, when he fell he put his foot through a basement window and the sound of breaking glass attracted the attention of priest inside.

CHAPTER THIRTY-TWO

Daphne called the number on the pamphlet. The telephone receptionist at the abortion clinic was courteous and professional. She asked Daphne basic questions without prying. She suggested counseling with one of the clinic doctors as a starting point and gave her an appointment later in the afternoon.

Daphne was told to come with an escort and cautioned to avoid the protestors outside the clinic building. I agreed to be her escort and we arrived at the clinic at the appointed time.

The protestors were on us before we could park. They shouted, waved grotesque signs, and tried to shove pamphlets through our car windows. After we had parked, they blocked the sidewalk and we had to walk in the street. Some were reading loudly from the bible, some were repeating the rosary and some were shouting prepared slogans printed on the backs of the signs given to them by protest leaders. There was a police officer near the door and I asked him why the protestors weren't being arrested for harassing people coming in and out of the building.

"This is a big building," I stated. "There must be other tenants inside beside the clinic, why are these fanatics allowed to act like this?

"You're right." the Officer replied. "There are a lot of other offices in the building and the protestors have no way to knowing who is going to a chiropractor a dentist, a doctor or the abortion clinic, so rather than ask, they got into everyone's face."

Running a gauntlet of insults and threats from disheveled and hysterical fanatics was unnerving and the Officer cautioned us that they would try to evoke a physical response from anyone they could.

"They will try to get you to touch them. Then they fake an injury, claim they have been assaulted, and demand I arrest you. Unfortunately, I'm not allowed to stop them unless they trespass or actually touch someone. Any other group that presented bloody signs and made threats would be disbursed or arrested, but abortion protestors bring their religious claims with them and use religion to intimidate the law."

"They look dangerous." Daphne commented.

"In general they are just a loud annoyance." the Officer responded. "But there are some among them that are dangerous and sometimes they get carried away. They have bombed and burned clinics, killed doctors and nurses and they photograph everyone they think is getting an abortion. They copy down license plates and post 'dead or alive' wanted posters on the internet and still they claim they are doing God's work in a nonviolent way. Some of the protestors are homeless street people paid to stand here, oh, and be careful what you say to them, they record you and use snippets from your comments to recruit more fanatics and to discredit you if they can. If they record you, be assured you will be on a screen in some church basement as a symbol of evil within the week. "Hell," the Officer bragged, "I'm a church basement movie star."

Inside the clinic, I was surprised to see a modern medical facility. I commented on how clean and comfortable the clinic was and the receptionist informed me that, in spite of the propaganda from protestors, Abortion clinics were fully licensed as outpatient surgical centers and everyone on staff had to meet the same standards as any doctor or surgery center employee. Daphne explained to the receptionist that she was uncertain as to her options and had an appointment to talk to a counselor and a doctor. The receptionist explained that counseling was a prerequisite for any procedure and that she would not be encouraged to have an abortion. The decision was entirely hers.

"The choice is yours alone." The receptionist said. "We just want to be sure you are aware of all your options, including adoption."

While we waited, I noticed the diversity of other women in the waiting room. There were very young girls not much older than my daughter. Some were with their mothers and others with boy friends. There were also middle-aged women of all races and from various economic backgrounds, but especially the poor. Several suspect couples made me question if the women were there voluntarily. Could they be victims of the Minister's rampage, forced to abort a supposed alien child? It was a chilling thought.

I also wondered what would happen to the protestors if alien seed myths persisted. If the myths persisted, the radicals demonstrating in front of the building in opposition to abortion could easily switch sides and begin demonstrating for forced abortions.

My musings were cut short when Daphne's name was called.

CHAPTER THIRTY-THREE

The castrated minister was very lucky. Thanks to an alert priest, he reached the hospital in time to stop the bleeding and received life saving transfusions.

Safe within his hospital room the minister had time to reflect. The news he watched on his hospital room TV was making him question both the alien prime number theory and the DNA alteration evidence. If there had been no alien visitation, and if his DNA had not been affected, he was just a fool, a fool that had been seduced by the assumption that he had been chosen as a sacred vessel for a second coming.

Now, he was faced with the possibility that there had been no factual basis for his behavior. He had lost both his genitalia and his moral compass, and as his physical wounds healed, his depression deepened.

Because the minister had been the victim of attempted murder he was placed in a secure wing of the hospital and had visitors restricted. Other than police interrogating him about the attack in the cemetery, and FBI agents interrogating him about his multi state sperm-selling spree, he had few visitors. The one exception was the priest that had found him in the window well. Father Mathew was always kind and always brought a single fresh flower from the church' garden.

"Just like all of life," Father Mathew would say as he put a fresh flower into the bud vase on the Minister's bedside table, "There are seasons, and the bloom will sometimes disappear, but if we believe and if we are patient it will return."

The minister appreciated Father Mathew's metaphor but needed more than kind words to convince him his life could ever be normal again.

"I like the parable, Father, and believe I will be resurrected, but how do I atone for the mistakes I have made. If the myths are true, I may have been the instrument of the Devil and spread his seed. If the myths are only myths, I have misled many for my own gain and have created false gods that many now worship."

Father Mathew smiled.

"And if the myths are true or false, and even if you thought you were doing the work of God, you really surrendered only to greed and it became your master. Your only sin is greed and you aren't responsible for others that serve the myths for their own reasons. Repent your greed with humility and when you find a way to give back, you will find atonement"

The Minister tried to recall all of his stops at fertility clinics for the FBI, but there had been many and he hadn't kept any records. He was told that if he cooperated he might receive a lesser sentence. But he didn't know what he was charged with, and his interrogators either didn't know or wouldn't tell him.

He had never lied to those paying him for his sperm and never claimed that the tree sap had altered his DNA. The scar in his hand and inconclusive tests, hyped by the press were enough to create the demand, and as his interrogators seemed more interested in the clinics and doctors that had re-sold his sperm than in him.

Feeling uncomfortable with the way he was being questioned and not being able to get any definite answers as to his legal status, he asked for a lawyer. The next day a tall man with a brief case and gray hair came into his hospital room and introduced himself.

"I'm Jason Madden, your lawyer."

With legal representation, the minister learned that he had broken no laws. The clinics, however, had misrepresented the sperm they sold and made claims they couldn't back up. The Minister was cleared of all charges. He had never claimed to carry alien seed and was seen as a victim of mass hysteria.

CHAPTER THIRTY-FOUR

After waiting in the reception area for what seemed to be a long time, Daphne returned from her counseling. She paid her bill and motioned for me to follow her. As we left the building, we were confronted by the relentless abortion protestors a second time, and again, had to walk in the street to reach the car.

"That was a bit frightening." I said as I dodged the last protestor who tried to cover my windshield with a poster. "I hope your session with the doctor was less stressful?"

"It was." Daphne answered. "They encouraged me not to have an abortion unless I was absolutely certain and made me realize that I have a few more months to make up my mind. They weren't surprised that I found their brochure in the chapel and told me their Director speaks often at hospitals, to church groups, and at schools, not to encourage abortions, but to encourage behavior that would make them unnecessary. I was impressed with the courage and professionalism of their staff. They certainly aren't the murderers that nasty crowd outside claims they are, and they have to face those terrorists on the sidewalk every day."

"So you have decided to postpone your decision, at least for now?"

"No, I've decided. I'm going to have the baby and I don't want any complications from Floyd. I need your help in getting him out of the picture. I want the baby to be totally separated from Floyd and Floyd's tree. So far only you and I know that Floyd is the father and I would like to keep it that way."

I had to think for a moment before I answered.

"Legally we can get Floyd to relinquish his parental rights and possibly to voluntarily agree to a gag order so no one ever knows your child was sired by him, but you will be forfeiting any claims for child support. Getting practical separation from your own celebrity status as a primary news reporter on Floyd's trial and Floyd's tree is going to be a bit more difficult, unless you want to change your name and start a completely new life."

"That's not a bad Idea." Daphne replied. "I could use a new life and my baby deserves to grow up without my past casting any shadows. How difficult is it to change one's name?"

"Legally you need a good reason to justify the change, which might involve having to reveal the father of your child, but there is an easier way, just get married."

"So what do I do? Put an ad in the paper, lonely woman with child needs husband for name change only."

Daphne was serious but I couldn't help but laugh.

"That wasn't quite what I had in mind"

"What did you have in mind? I only have a few more months before I begin to show and questions begin to be asked. The only men I have associated with since all this began is you and Floyd. Julia probably suspects that Floyd and I had a fling. Floyd's Doctor couldn't help but notice that I had a crush on Floyd, and your daughter is a lot smarter than you think. It won't be long before someone figures this out, and if you think those right-to-life protestors were bad, you haven't been following the news. Did you see what they did to Floyd's Minister? These new cults are crazy and would kill me and the baby in a heartbeat."

I thought for a moment.

"If you marry, the marriage needs to be kept quiet and only those already involved need to be a part of it. They are the only ones you can trust to keep your secret."

"So I can't join a dating service, can't meet some neat guy in a bar, and if I do find someone in the next month or so, I will have to lie to him from the start. Your name change idea is beginning to stink. I can't marry Floyd. That will only make things worse, besides Floyd is already committed to Douglas. That leaves you and the Minister and I doubt if the minister is interested in marriage and is probably still on the cults hit list. That leaves you"

Daphne was still serious but I couldn't help but find her logic funny.

"Was that a proposal," I quipped.

"I don't know." Daphne answered. "Maybe, it does make sense. It's a story people could believe."

I couldn't help but mock her logic.

"That has to be the most desperate proposal of marriage ever made. "Please marry me before I turn into a tree."

"You're not funny." She said, and began to cry.

I had been insensitive and I hated myself for it. She was desperately trying to escape from a trap I had created. I was turning her desperation into a joke, and I wasn't sure why? I pulled the car to the curb and shut off the engine.

"I'm sorry," I said. "That was mean and insensitive. Instead of trying to help, I was protecting myself."

"Since my wife died I have felt guilty about even noticing a pretty woman, and you have made me feel guilty more than once. I was jealous of Floyd but glad he needed me as his lawyer so I could stay close to you. I suppose that's the real reason I suggested the trip to New York."

"Jenny is smart, you're right. She has asked me several times how I felt about you and even told me that it was obvious that I liked you, and I do, but I felt like a desperate older man chasing a much younger woman."

"Not that much younger," Daphne replied. "And now there is a desperate younger woman reaching out to a not so much older man. Does every marriage have to begin with love and passion? Why can't it be based on logic or even desperation? You're lonely, I'm desperate and Jenny needs a mother. We don't have to share a bed, if that makes it easier for you, but I need a new name for my child, a safe place to live and a way to start over. You could be a father to a newborn again and Jenny could be a big sister. It's a lot to ask but I have no other options."

Daphne stopped talking, took my hand, looked into my eyes and waited for an answer.

CHAPTER THIRTY-FIVE

Floyd's paintings sold for much more than expected and his financial future became instantly secure. His transition from a farmer to a sophisticated painter had made him rich, but it had also quelled his obsession to paint. He was a new man, but a man without a vocation. Fortunately, the truly rich have no trouble finding other ways to contribute, and Floyd was no exception.

The news of the attack on Floyd's Minister spread quickly. The reports called the attack attempted murder but left out the details. Floyd felt responsible for all of the events that had fallen from the tree. He had given the tree status by making it the center of his stories, he had let his father take a fatal ride on a snowmobile, and had lost control and caused his grandmother's heart attack.

The myths and the hysteria were not of his making but if he had not kept the ancient myths alive, the tree might be setting peacefully next to the soybean patch instead of under a giant inflatable dome. He couldn't undo any of it, but with the help of Douglas, he was dealing with his guilt and searching for ways to make amends.

Floyd had no knowledge of Daphne's pregnancy and Daphne was thankful, but Floyd's remorse was drawing him back to Ohio. Floyd's Minister had survived the deadly chain of events that Floyd had set in motion and Floyd felt compelled to talk to him.

Floyd located the hospital where his former Minister was recuperating, traveled to the location and went inside. It took some time for the hospital staff to verify Floyd's need to visit, but eventually he was allowed into the minister's room.

At first, the minister didn't recognize the well-dressed man standing at his bedside, but when Floyd turned exposing his mask, he recognized him immediately.

"Floyd. Is that you?"

"Yes reverend it's me. I heard of your ordeal and I had to see you. I'm so sorry. If it hadn't been for me, you wouldn't be here. I'm so very sorry."

"It wasn't your fault."

The minister reached out to Floyd to comfort him.

"I believed the stories the scientists told and got myself into this predicament by being greedy. My commitment to narrow religious beliefs made me vulnerable to the myths and the stories of messages from beyond earth and the symbolic scar in my hand made me delusional. The people that hurt me were suffering from similar delusions. I have forgiven them and you should forgive yourself. You were delusional when you attacked the tree. Myths, even religious myths can drive any of us mad. We need to believe with caution."

Floyd was surprised

"You preach a very different message than I remember from attending your church. Have you lost your faith?"

The minister laughed. "I'm surprised you remember anything from my sermons. You didn't seem very attentive and you didn't come to my church very often. No, I haven't lost my faith but it has changed. What about you Floyd? You seem very different from the Floyd I knew on the farm."

The man in the mask and the man of God talked for more than an hour. The tree and its myths had profoundly affected them both, and had given them common ground. Near the end of their discussion, they talked of the future and Floyd had an idea.

"Reverend, the new myths from the tree may or may not be true. Doubt is growing about the prime numbers being alien, and they think they have identified the species of the tree, but new religions have sprung from other older myths and they persist in spite of recent doubts. Some of the new religions are harmless and fanciful and some are dangerous. You understand this better than anyone does. If you had a church could you bring reason to these new myths and try to make them safe and maybe even valuable?"

The minister remained silent. His search for a way to give back and atone for his sins suddenly seemed within reach. Floyd and the minister talked for hours about their similar transformations, about their new insights and about the possibility of bringing ancient beliefs and scientific discoveries together under a shared umbrella of beliefs.

Over the next few days, with the help of Father Mathew, Floyd and his minister developed an outline for a belief system that included both the magnificence of the discoveries of modern science and the sanctity of the church. There were disagreements on details, but none of them challenged the idea that a creator, or at least a guiding impetus, had brought the basic elements of creation together in predetermined patterns, and that life and awareness were included as ultimate outcomes.

Floyd avoided a legal battle over his property rights by donating all but twenty acres of his farm to The Ohio State University for use by their agricultural research department. The twenty-acre parcel he retained included the old farmhouse and the barn, which he turned into a working museum to honor farm life and his father. The rest of the twenty acres he donated to the new church he created for the minister. He had a large inflatable dome, similar to the one covering the tree, erected to serve as the church sanctuary and installed the injured minister as its head. While working with Floyd to formalize its denomination and to create the legal foundation for the church, it was inevitable that he would learn that Daphne and I were engaged. He was delighted.

Other than Floyd, Jenny had been Daphne's and my primary concern, and we delayed the announcement of our engagement until we were certain my daughter felt comfortable with the idea. She would have a new mother and a younger brother or sister. Jenny was stoic at first but came around quickly when we determined that Daphne's child was a boy. When Jenny was offered the opportunity to help choose her younger brother's name, she became doubly enthusiastic.

Jenny kept Daphne's pregnancy secret until Floyd could be approached and until we could formalize his forfeiture of parental rights by naming the father of the unborn as uncertain, and to remain undetermined. Floyd's only request was that we consider being married in his new church with his minister presiding. We had originally wanted to keep our marriage secret by using a justice of the peace, but Floyd's request made more sense, as long as he kept the ceremony a private affair.

Daphne and I were married under the new dome in a quiet but strange ceremony. Floyd acted as best man. Julia was Daphne's maid of honor. Jenny acted as flower girl and carried a silver spoon on a small velvet pillow as a token of our commitment to each other.

With pets and farm animals as witnesses, Floyd's minister pronounced us man and wife.

All of us had our secrets. Jenny surmised most of them, but knew she had to hold them as sacred trusts or risk her new family. Jenny's brother was born healthy and as Jenny jokingly said, "thankfully without leaves or thorns".

Jenny was wise for her years, and helped take care of her brother and loved him dearly. All of the secrets from under the multiple domes on the Brenner farm were kept. No one questioned the new scientific discoveries, and. no one questioned the paternity of Daphne's child.

Jenny knew instinctively that her brother had a gay father, and still believed most of the stories told about the tree, including those regarding its alien DNA. She couldn't help but wonder if her younger brother's DNA had been affected.

Jenny spent a considerable amount of time selecting a good name for her brother never thinking Daphne would actually use the name she suggested.

Not realizing she was selecting the name of the father of modern medicine, Jenny indulged in a bit of childish humor, and came up with a tongue-in-cheek name for her stepbrother by creating an acronym for; "The Gay Alien".

She would never let anyone know how she had arrived at Galen's name. It would be her secret forever.

END